About the Author

Arianne Richmonde is the *USA TODAY* bestselling author of suspense novel *Stolen Grace,* and the contemporary romance Pearl Series—*Shades of Pearl, Shadows of Pearl, Shimmers of Pearl, Pearl,* and *Belle Pearl.* Arianne is an American author who was raised in both the US and Europe and now lives in France with her husband and coterie of animals. She used to be an actress and ***Shooting Star*** is inspired by her past career—she is a huge fan of TV, film, and theatre and loves nothing better than a great performance.

Acknowledgements

Thank you, Nelle, for keeping me going each day. And Dee, Gloria, Letty, Cheryl, and Paula. Paul my amazing formatter at BB eBooks – who has saved me from several meltdowns because he is always there for me. And to my incredible readers and fans. Always yours – you inspire me.

Shooting Star

(A Beautiful Chaos book)

by

ARIANNE RICHMONDE

This is the first book in the
Beautiful Chaos Trilogy:

Shooting Star

Falling Star

Shining Star

FEB 2017

You must have chaos within you to give birth to a dancing star.

Friedrich Nietzsche

T HE FIRST THING EVERYBODY wanted
to know about me (apart from who I was
dating) was how the hell did a nineteen-year-old
get (a) so rich and (b) so screwed-up? I asked
myself the same thing, daily. When I glanced at
myself in a passing mirror I'd say, *Hey Star, what
happened? And when? When exactly was it that things got
so . . . so chaotic?* And what, girl, are you going to do
about it? I often wondered how I'd been so lucky,
but I also took it all for granted. The way movie
stars generally do when they feel fame is their
birthright.

Still, I was no fool, every day I counted my

lucky stars and knew that at any given click of God's big fat thumb and index finger, all this could be taken away from me.

Not that I was some religious God freak. I could count the times I'd been to church on one hand. But when the chips were down I found myself making deals with God. And after I'd hit an all-time low at rehab, I promised God—the last night I was there, in fact—that I'd be a good girl if he could just procure that part for me. The role I'd had my eye on.

The role I was born to play: Skye in *Skye's The Limit.*

Most people think that actors are super-confident. But no. We're all terrified. Terrified that we'll be out of a job. That the last big success was a fluke—that we'll be discovered as phonies. And that someone more beautiful, more talented or more something-or-other will topple us from our pedestals. The truth is, we *are* fakes. All of us. That's the nature of our job. We lie. We trick people into believing we are someone else. When we cry, sometimes it's real and other times an act. And nobody can tell the difference. We're so good at what we do that we even fool ourselves.

Especially ourselves.

We glimmer on the red carpet. We are glorious. Victorious—but we're also walking time bombs. Waiting to detonate. Waiting for our secret to be revealed. The big secret being that *we're no better than anybody else.*

We get zits. We look like shit before Hair and Make-up gets their hands on us. People dump us. Hey, even Marilyn Monroe was treated like crap by various men.

Even goddam, luminescent, Marilyn freakin' Monroe.

And although I wasn't aware of it then, I was as vulnerable as Marilyn when I walked out of that clinic and stepped—in my Choos—into a velvet-carpeted limo, purring like a welcoming pussycat, waiting to take me away from the ugly world of imperfection, back to my cocoon of beautiful chaos, that shone so brilliantly on the outside—like a floating bubble that mirrored a cerulean-blue sky and the sun which glittered its golden rays—blinding all my fans.

That wonderful, hopeful May afternoon, I knew I was *back.*

Back to conquer Hollywood.

PRODUCTION
Shooting Star

DIRECTOR
Jake Wild

DATE
May

SCENE
In the car

TAKE
2

CAMERA
Jake Wild

"**Y**OU'RE NOT SERIOUS?" I asked, my jaw on the floor. "You're joking?"

Brian carried on calmly chewing gum, the cloying aroma of Juicy Fruit wafting about his Porsche like air freshener. He sank deeper into his seat, his large body oozing with self-satisfied confidence, or what I suspected to be a little fart— although it could have been the new leather of the seat squeaking. "Jake," he said, "you'll thank me for this later."

"There won't be a 'later,'" I shot back, my voice rising. "Because there's no fucking way I'm having that . . . that . . . liability on legs in my movie!"

"She's fresh out of rehab. She's turned the page."

"Yeah, for how long? Twenty-four hours? My leading lady needs to give the performance of a lifetime in *Skye's The Limit*, not be snorting charlie in her dressing room. This is not some brainless blockbuster, Brian, this is *art*!"

"There's nothing more artistic than the creation of money, Jake. She's box office. Now, more than ever. You know how much airtime she gets? How many times a day she graces the news, or her photo's in some magazine?"

"Yeah, but for all the wrong reasons. My answer is no. N-O. No."

Brian picked the gum out from his rubbery lips and stuck it in a Kleenex. He smirked and said nothing. Then crunched the tissue in his fist like a boxer preparing for a punch. His jaw tightened. Little veins popped in his forehead like blue tributaries of a river. "You'll work with her," he said solemnly, the smirk now edging into a Robert de Niro sneer; the sneer Bob's bad characters don when they're about to do something crazy.

"Why? Why are you so obsessed with putting her in my film? There are other A-list actresses who would kill for the role of Skye. Why Star fucking Davis?"

"She's hot. She's beautiful."

"She'll come to the set drunk, high on pills, her entourage trailing behind her like slimy snails leaving behind a residue of—"

"It's done," Brian said, cutting me off. "She's signed. *We've* signed. I'm the producer and I'm calling the shots here."

"*What?*" I yelled.

"Don't raise your voice. Okay, it wasn't me who decided. It was the person I have to answer to."

"Who's that?"

"HookedUp Enterprises, who is mostly backing this. Pearl Chevalier was determined that Star was right for the part. Which meant she had her husband behind her, telling me to tow the line and abide by Pearl's wishes."

"I thought they'd sold up."

"She still has her fingers in all the Hooked Up

Enterprise pies. My hands were tied, Jake."

I took a breath and counted to ten. Well, tried to count to ten but broke out at six, "What's the catch?" Silence. Brian looked down at his fleshy knuckles and a sheepish flicker of guilt spread across his puffy face that spelled *I had no choice*. "What's the catch, Brian? I demanded again. "No sane producer is going to take a risk like that without some sort of payoff."

"She's coming in under budget."

"What the fuck's that supposed to mean?"

"You know when you take a date out to dinner and she's like the most beautiful woman in the room? And you're broke but you want to impress her?"

Brian was anything but broke. I wasn't sure where this conversation was heading.

"And you think she's going to order caviar or something and you're worrying about how you're going to pay the check?—and then she actually says she wants a soda and a salad and you're like, thank fucking God."

"You're telling me Star Davis just wants a soda? I don't think so." The last thing I read about

Star Davis was that she only drank Cristal. From 1930s champagne saucers, no less. 'Simple' wasn't her style.

"She's basically doing this part for free," Brian explained.

"But she commands millions. Twenty million, wasn't it? Her last movie?"

"She was desperate for the part of Skye. She knows it's the role of a lifetime."

"She's doing it for *no pay?*"

"Practically. A couple hundred thousand dollars. That's free in her language."

I shook my head. "She's wrong for the part."

"She's right for the part and you know it."

I scraped my hands anxiously through my hair. "I can't let this happen. This is insane. *Insane!*"

"It's done, Jake. That was the deal. You got creative control except for casting. It's done and dusted. Your granddaddy and your uncle can't do a thing about it now so don't think you can pull the 'Hollywood Royalty' card and get them involved in this."

Blood rushed to my ears. I wanted to punch him square in the face. But what Brian said was true, although I was loath to admit it and even ashamed on some level. Not ashamed of my granddad or uncle or my father. Hell, no. With seven Oscars between them they were as respected and acclaimed as any film director or producer could be. And I loved them. But a deep-rooted humiliation lodged at the pit of my stomach like a lump of food you've swallowed too fast—I'd been born with a shiny golden spoon in my mouth. Rich and privileged my whole damn life. Eternally trying to prove that I merited my present success. That I wasn't some spoiled British brat basking in the rays of Hollywood nepotism. In fact, my father hadn't given me a penny since my eighteenth birthday and I was a wealthy man in my own right even though I was still only twenty-six. Had four movies under my belt, all directed by yours truly, one of which had been nominated the year before for a Golden Globe for best screenplay (which I co-wrote and produced). Still, the "lucky bastard-has-never-had-to-do-a hard-day's-work-in-his-life" label left a chip on my shoulder. A notch out of the smooth marble gleam that was my indisputable success. I was being given a fifty-seven million dollar budget for *Skye's The Limit*. Nobody hands out that sort of cash to someone who hasn't proven himself and I was no exception. But it came with strings attached and I felt like a marionette dancing for the big, Hollywood puppet masters.

"Look," Brian said, his chubby fingers barely touching the steering wheel as we cruised along. "It's not just me. This town's being run by conglomerates and corporations now, not individuals, you know that. They don't give a crap about anything but big bucks and returns. These suits don't care about art. They want 'bums on seats' as you Brits say. My advice? Shut the fuck up about Star, do your job and you'll be nominated for Best Director this time next year."

I shook my head. "You've really asked for trouble casting her, you know that, don't you?"

"She won an *Oscar,* Jake. She can *act.*"

I laughed. "She was nine years old, Brian! Since then her greatest jobs have been *blow* jobs."

"Now you're being crude."

He shoved another stick of Juicy Fruit in his gob and buzzed down his window. A warm spring breeze blew welcomingly into the car. "Why have I got the air-con going?" he said with a chuckle. "It's a beautiful day outside." He fiddled with the music control on the steering wheel and Amy Winehouse's "Rehab" blared out. His idea of a joke, obviously.

"I can't believe you did that," I mumbled.

"Rolled the window down or play this song?"

"Star Davis," I said. *"Really?"*

"There was no point telling you. I knew you'd never agree."

"I should walk away right now. Leave you to stew in your own juices—you can find some other mug director who'll take her on."

"Maybe, but I know you won't do that. You have too much of your soul already invested in this picture."

I looked out of the open window as Los Angeles crawled past in the traffic and exhaled a sigh of momentary defeat. This town was doing my head in. Making me lose sight of reality. The palm trees towering into the azure sky like skinny skyscrapers reaching as high as they could go— everyone reaching beyond their means. Grabbing, aspiring, grasping, taking. Even the trees, goddammit. And the houses on Sunset with their manicured lawns, making you believe that life could be controlled, clipped, neatened. Like my father. A control freak who'd move a pencil one inch to the left if he felt it was out of place. Not on set, no. In his own freaking home! A pencil. And I tried to be like him. Organized. Sharp. On the ball. Controlled. A colonel-in-the-army type. But that wasn't me and never had been. I secretly welcomed madness with relish. Unintentionally courted it. Nurtured dysfunction as if it were a breastfeeding baby, willing chaos into my life the way some people attract money or women. Right now my mind was rattling with a sort of hectic glee. Star Davis represented turmoil and for some unknown reason it excited me—my curiosity piqued.

"I wanted an *unknown* for the role of Skye," I told Brian, willing my thoughts back to safer waters. *A nice, new actress with no baggage, no ego and no "history"—that's what I need.* "I've been auditioning at drama schools all over the world. I've seen sixty-two actresses. I'd narrowed it down to eight. And now you tell me I've basically wasted my time?"

"You tell the press that very same thing. 'I saw sixty-two actresses and, you know what? None of them hold a candle to Star Davis.' "

"A candle that's going to start a fire."

"You'll figure it out, Jake. I mean, let's face it, she's met her match—*match*, haha, no pun intended, Get it? She can set you alight."

I didn't laugh at his joke. "What's that supposed to mean, 'met her match'?"

"Bad boy Jake Wild—you've had some good times on the casting couch yourself, my friend. You can't deny you've clocked up quite a reputation over the years."

"The couch has been reupholstered, Brian. The past is the *past*. I don't take advantage of starry-eyed actresses these days. I'm a professional. I get the job done and don't screw around with the talent anymore. Ever. Well, as of last week. It's my number one rule."

"Well leave Star in peace, you know what I'm saying? She's vulnerable. She's fresh out of rehab and needs to be *looked after*." He fixed his piggy gaze on me, a bushy eyebrow twitching ironically.

"Oh no! Don't look at me, mate. There's no way I'll be her fucking nanny!"

"You're the only one, Jake, who can keep her on the straight and narrow. We can't have her going AWOL in the middle of a shoot. She'll need to be watched like a hawk."

"What about her sea of bodyguards? her PA, her father, for that matter?"

"None of them can be trusted. She's too manipulative. Besides, they're all on her payroll."

"Her father too?"

"He's her unofficial manager."

"Great 'manager,' " I murmured.

"Star's been supporting her entire family ever since she did that diaper commercial when she was two years old. She has a strange perspective on life. She has never been told 'no.' So she's used to being boss, and getting what she wants."

"Well she's not bloody bossing me." I said that with bravado, yet here I was being 'bossed' by the system. Brian. The executive producers, the producers, the moneymen, the money women . . . the goddam accountants. The suits whose faces I'd never even seen. And indirectly, Star herself. She'd slithered her way into winning the part of Skye with her wily ways, by offering herself practically free. Clever girl. She'd probably sucked someone's dick to get the part. She had me in a corner and I hadn't even met her yet.

"And one more thing," Brian added. "Apparently her house is about to be remodeled and she was planning to move into a hotel for a while. But I don't trust the idea of Star Davis running around loose in a hotel, you know? Too many distractions—too much booze on tap."

"What's your point?" I said, meeting his eyes with a stony glare.

"I thought until every shot is in the can it would be a good idea if she stayed in your home— you can make sure there're no temptations—no drugs or liquor anywhere near her."

I stared at him incredulously as he smoothly took a bend, the Porsche revving with a quiet growl.

He went on, "We can hire our own bodyguard—someone who can't be bribed by her to slip her anything—he could live in your guest house—the one in your garden? And *she* could stay in one of your guest bedrooms. So, you know, she'll be under your roof." He was serious when he said this.

"No. Brian, you're really pushing your luck. I have limits. I don't want some wayward teenager telling me to fuck off in my own house. I'm not her father. I'm a film director. I have *work* to do. Storyboards to prepare, scenes to plan out. I have to stay on top of the shooting schedule, liaise with my assistant director, my lighting cameraman— Jesus, what the fuck? I don't have *time* to deal with some drug-addicted, attention-seeking, Cristal-drinking brat!"

I felt trapped in his car, listening to his bullshit. But what could I do? It was my driver's day off. Half of Hollywood were acting as my chauffeurs since I'd had my license taken away from me six months before. I'd been over the limit (barely) but it had been 3 a.m., when there were hardly any cars on the road, so being hauled over by the LAPD was the last thing I'd been expecting. Brian was right: my reputation for being a bad boy was on par with Star's wild-child antics. We had indeed each met our match. Only, I really *had* turned over a new leaf, but Star Davis? *That would be the day.* I started ruminating on what actress we could hire when it all went—because I knew it would—badly pear-shaped. We'd need to have a Plan B. An understudy, the way they do with theatre productions. Someone who looked like her and could act—maybe we could use some of the same footage—back view shots anyway. . . . . .

"We're here." Brian shook me from my reverie as we drew up in front of my house. We'll talk later. Think about what I said."

"Right," I said sarcastically, and slammed the passenger door harder than I'd intended.

My 1920s mansion stood there, its white façade blanched to a glare in the harsh May sunlight. The lawn stretched before me like a smooth carpet. The gardener must have come because it was neat and smelled freshly mown. As beautiful as my home was, I intended to sell it and buy something more discreet in the Hills. I was becoming too well known to have a villa smack on Sunset Boulevard. I sniggered to myself, imagining the fiasco if Star came to live with me for the duration of the shoot. The paparazzi would have a fucking hay day. Impossible, Brian needed his head examined! What kind of crazy-fool idea was he hatching? To get me arrested along with her? For aiding and abetting an underage alcoholic? The USA's ridiculous age limit for drinking was twenty-one. Being British, I found this absurd. I'd been going to pubs since I was fifteen. Star was still only nineteen. "Illegal." A nineteen-year-old edging her way into my life when she was the last thing I needed. Fuck! Who was I fooling, believing I had things under control? Yes, I was a pretty powerful man in Hollywood, with the extra clout of my grandfather, dad and uncle behind me. And with more money than was sane. I owned two vacation homes, a luxury flat in London, a fleet of cars (which presently, I wasn't even bloody well able to drive) and artwork that belonged in museums. But I still had to answer to people. They had assured me—and I had it in my contract—I'd have creative control. But at that point I had no idea quite how damn "creative" things were about to get.

I SPOTTED JAKE WILD from across the room. Good looking. *Very* good looking. Messy dark blond hair that hung down over his brow and a busyness that I found appealing—a man on the move, confident, in control. A director who didn't flinch at fame and fortune because he wasn't treating his star cast like they were porcelain, like some directors do—the sycophantic approach which always ends up a disaster because the director has too much reverence for his actors to get on and *direct.* Jake was a pro and knew what he was doing; it was obvious by the way he felt so at ease with his cast. I smiled at him as I walked into the room but all he could say was, "You're late, Star."

I guessed what was going through his mind; that he didn't want me to play Skye. Well too bad. The part was *mine* and I was determined in that moment to show him what I was made of.

The read-through was nerve-wracking. All the heavyweights were there. Meryl, Bobby de Niro, and Ian McKellen, with his deep British drawl that made me regret instantly that I hadn't trained at drama school, and that I didn't know my trade to save my life. The *Breathe From The Diaphragm Darling* school of acting—when *my* kind of training was self-taught and 'on the job'—observing other actors at their craft, or watching old black and white movies past midnight, while eating pizza and drinking vodka, reading about Stanislavsky and the Method, high on another kind of method— Meth—or whatever I'd been able to lay my hands on. That was after I'd turned "bad," at the age of fourteen, a few years after Mom died. Before that I was a straight-A student, high IQ and all, and scarily precocious. I studied like crazy and even read Brecht and Pinter plays and wrote reams of pretentious poetry and learned chunks of Sylvia Plath off by heart.

But the cast was all so sweet to me. Nobody was playing king or queen, the way some actors do, like they have a rod up their ass or a lemon in their mouth. Nobody looked down on me. No, they were joking and laughing, making me feel like I was one of them. That we were a team—a family.

I sat at the table, the script in my hands, hoping that nobody could see how badly I was trembling. The whole reading was like a surreal dream. All I could think of was being perfect and not disappointing anyone; least of all, my director. By the time it came to the scene when I'm reunited with my father I was a wreck.

I thought of my own dad, let the anger build inside me—the memory of rehab, him being such a hopeless non-parent, for leaning on me—his own daughter—for financial support. I could see the other actors—legends all of them—and I felt overwhelmed: a plug being pulled in a bathtub and all the dirty water gushing down the hole, spiraling into a vacuum. That was me. I let it all out.

I glanced at my script and hissed out my line:

"Dad," I said. "Should I even call you that?" A lump knotted in my dry throat and I blinked hard, letting the tears that had been welling up fall down my face. But then I stoically sat up straight—to show Skye's pride—and added in a whisper, "No, you chicken-shit excuse for a father, you don't deserve that word."

I could feel Jake's eyes on me but I didn't look at him.

After we'd finished I could tell that Jake was astounded. Yes, *astounded*—I can't think of a better word to describe how his jaw hit the ground. Figuratively speaking. Before the read-through he'd hardly looked at me, like I was less important than, I don't know, the person sweeping the floor. But after the reading he came up to me. Laid his hand on my shoulder, but then quickly took it away as if he was afraid he might catch something, like I was contagious.

His eyes seemed to sparkle as he spoke. "That was good, Star. Really good. Can you bring that level of emotion to the set? I'd like to catch that intensity on the first take."

I'd heard that about him—that he was a

director who liked to rehearse off camera and then get the perfect shot within the first few takes. He'd done a lot of theatre and indie movies—he wasn't used to wasting celluloid on big budget films the way I was. His question was loaded. My last film was a fiasco. Between a director who had no control of his project, and me being high half the time, we were getting the shot on take thirty-two. Once, take eighty-one. That's expensive. And exhausting. But getting it perfect on the first take? That was a very tall order.

"Sure," I said casually. "Why not?" Although my heart was pounding—the pressure was on.

Jake narrowed his eyes and added, "Or was that a one-off?"

I felt heat rise in my stomach—a compliment followed by a stab to the gut. "I'm an actor, Jake. Don't worry, I'll do my job."

"You really held your own in there. They were impressed." But then he backtracked again and said, "Well not *impressed*, exactly. But, you know, relieved that . . . well, you're one of them. You're not just a movie star, not just a pretty face, put it that way."

"Right," I muttered. I couldn't think what else to reply. He was a jerk but a sexy one, and it infuriated me that I wanted to hate him but couldn't, because for some crazy reason my heart was beating faster than normal, my breath uneven. His gray-green eyes pierced me with a look that I couldn't quite read. Challenging me, daring me, but also admonishing me as if he were some sort of father figure—and me the naughty child. His jaw strong, his cheekbones defined like a character from an old novel; Jane Austen maybe—a face that was as beautiful as it was masculine. Not modern but from another era. But the way he was dressed made him look like any other Hollywood type; buffed up muscles toned from exercise, and a twenty-first century stance, with his legs firmly astride. Cocky, self-assured. Sexy as hell. His T–shirt loose and faded, and the edge of a beautifully crafted lion tattoo peaked out from beneath his hard bicep. I forced my gaze away. I didn't need him to feel any better about himself than he already did.

Jake's eyes suddenly frosted into an unexpected, chilling glare; he leaned forward and

whispered in my ear—shivers ran up my spine—
"So how *did* you get the part, Star?" he said
conspiratorially, as if there was no way I deserved
it, as if I had tricked them into hiring me. Fucked a
producer, maybe.

I looked up at the ceiling in exasperation and
tapped my foot, irritated at his gall, his disbelief in
me as an actor. "I won an Oscar once upon a time,
you know," I snapped back.

"You can't wear that crown of laurels forever,
Star." His English accent punched out the word
forever. "You'll need to work twice as hard as
anyone else on this film to prove yourself. I'm not
going to lie; I'll be tough on you. I don't intend to
mollycoddle you and tell you how great you are
every five minutes, okay? I know you're used to
kid-glove treatment but you won't get that from
me. Is that clear? It's not because I'm being unfair,
it's because this part is a golden opportunity for
you—maybe the last chance you'll ever get, roles
like these don't grow on trees—a golden
opportunity to show the world what you can do.
And you'd better come up with the goods when
the camera's rolling and not be off glugging down

Absolut somewhere, disguised in a Perrier bottle, sprawled out in your trailer, or worse—on set—as you've been known to do."

Wow, this guy could hit below the belt. "Oh ye of little faith," I said with a shrug as if his words meant nothing. And I must have rolled my eyes again because he replied:

"Stop with the teenage behavior, Star. You're better than that."

I was trying to remain cool but his harsh words made me snap, "Oh, like you're such a grown-up, model citizen *yourself*, Mr. Drink and Drive."

A muscle in Jake's jaw twitched like I'd struck a nerve. "Look, I wasn't even drunk," he said in a very low voice so nobody could hear, "I was avoiding a coyote running across the road. I was practically *sober* and the only reason I got stopped was because there was this *cop* crawling up my arse who had a bee in his bonnet about me and was determined to give me a hard time. He was following me like a bloodhound—knew who I was and wanted to teach me a lesson. Waiting for his moment—for his fifteen minutes of fame so his buddies back at the station would slap him on the back."

I laughed. "Welcome to the club! I get followed twenty-four-seven. I have to say I do like your line, 'practically sober.' That's a really good one. And the coyote? The kind of story I might invent. You should try a spot of rehab yourself, Jake. It might make you get off your high horse and see yourself for what you really are."

"And what am I?"

"An arrogant asshole," I said, and walked off, my heels clicking as I went, my long blond hair swinging as I tossed my head and lifted my chin into the air. I'd show that conceited jerk that I could act. He'd be eating out of my hand in no time.

PRODUCTION
Shooting Star

DIRECTOR
Jake Wild

DATE
May

SCENE
The read-through

TAKE
4

CAMERA
Jake Wild

W HEN SHE WALKED into the read-through and I set eyes on her for the first time ever in the flesh, a bolt of electricity shot through me like I had been struck by lightning. I wasn't expecting that. Not. One. Bit. I've seen enough stunning women in my life that usually I'm non-plussed. Of all the people in the world I was—and still am—the last person to be affected by movie star delirium. I've met hundreds of them over the years. Angelina and Brad, Al Pacino, Bob Redford. I sat on Cary Grant's knee when I was a baby, played chess with Dustin, hung out at the

Grand Prix in Monaco with Tom, lunch with Leonardo in Cannes—you name it, I've done it. Fame doesn't faze me in the slightest because I grew up on movie sets and these people have been part of my everyday life.

But when Star Davis slipped quietly into the room, wearing skinny jeans and a baggy sweater—not even any make-up—my heart literally missed a beat. She looked at me and smiled and in that smile I saw such vulnerability and such wickedness rolled into one that I knew we were soul mates. The look in her gaze said *I've got your number, buddy, don't fuck with me* and, *We're the same, you and I, and fate has brought us together.* Her long blond hair hung around her shoulders and her Robin's Egg Blue eyes penetrated right through me. Stunning. None of the photos I'd seen of her, nor even any of her films portrayed her sheer magnetism. I was charged with anticipation and excitement. It was like some visceral force was pulling us together. Blood rushed through my veins, awakening every cell in my body, my heart hammered in my chest. She was born to play Skye and I knew right then that Star was *my* responsibility. It was up to me to get an Oscar-worthy performance out of her and if I didn't it would be my failing, not hers.

But all I could come up with was, "You're late, Skye." I had a habit of calling actors by their character's name. It sometimes helped them identify more with the part. Or maybe I didn't call her Skye but just Star. "Sit down with the others at the table—they're waiting for you. Have you been over your script?"

"You'll see," she answered enigmatically, and then strutted in her high heels with great confidence to where all the other actors were, and instead of going around to introduce herself to everyone individually, she blew them a Marilyn kiss and then said, "I'm Star, by the way, and none of you need to tell me your names because you've all been hanging out with me my whole life. In my living room."

Everybody laughed and I breathed a sigh of relief. I could tell they already liked her and my only problem now? Was keeping temptation of every kind well away from her.

Myself included.

"SO WHAT'S HE LIKE?" Janice asked as she arranged a huge bouquet of white lilies in a vase, picking off leaves here and there and inhaling the overpowering aroma that was floating about my upstairs living room. Flowers arrived all the time from fans, or actor friends just wanting to say hi, or agents trying to poach me, or producers trying to woo me with a project. Janice was clucking about organizing my day—she was my assistant—my right arm as well as one of my most trusted friends, although she was older than me by eight years—used to be my babysitter, when Mom was too out of it to deal with me. Janice was womanly; always had been, even when she was just thirteen. Tall and confident, high cheekbones and feline-shaped eyes that glinted flinty-dark and made people respect her. I felt handicapped without Janice. She did everything for me. I'd once even had a car accident and both my wrists ended up in plaster. I won't get into the nitty-gritty details but you can imagine how much she helped me out.

"He's an arrogant prick," I said, as I lay stretched out on the sofa, with the script of *Skye's The Limit* held up above my head. We were listening to Will Pharrell's "Happy." And I did feel happy. Finally my life seemed to be coming together. "Okay, tell me which sounds better: 'I told you I was no good,' or like this: 'I told you I was no *good*!' "

"Who are you talking to at that point?"

"The guy I corrupt, the sixteen-year-old. He's kind of like the Leonardo character in *What's Eating Gilbert Grape*, you know? Mentally handicapped? And I make him run away with me and he's in love with me so does anything I say."

"You have sex with him in the movie?"

"No way! He's, you know, like drooling and

stuff. But he's sweet."

"Who's playing him?"

"This new actor that nobody's heard of yet. This is going to be big for him—it's an amazing part."

"So he was at the read-through the other day?"

"No, he's still in London. He's finishing up a play in the West End. I mean, when I say 'nobody's heard of him' he's huge in England, in the theatre world. Everybody's talking about how talented he is—I forget his name though."

"Cute talented, or like, just talented?"

"He's a baby. Only seventeen. Maybe one day he'll be cute but for now he's just plain talented."

"So who's Meryl playing?"

"The psycho prison warden."

"And Ian McKellen?—he's the Lord of the Rings guy, isn't he?"

"My grandfather."

"De Niro?"

"A cameo role: a peeping Tom pervert who I murder in the first scene."

"So your character is pretty fucked up?"

"Well, yeah. I mean, she's a serial killer so I

guess you'd say that's pretty fucked up. Although in a weird way I identify with her, you know?"

"You say that about all the parts you play—that's what makes you a good actress. This is *so* going to be the perfect role for you, Star."

I squinted my eyes at Janice. Sun was pouring through the huge picture window, lighting up her thick red hair like a halo. "Yup, that's why I moved mountains to get the role," I said.

I'd gotten my hands on the script via my agent's sister's assistant, who, in turn, had sneakily scanned a few pages when the script was fresh but hadn't been sent out yet. I prepared the shoot. Hired a studio for the day and got an actor friend to do the scene with me. I paid the best make-up artist in Hollywood to bruise me up (as was required at that point in the script), an amazing lighting cameraman I'd once worked with on an Oliver Stone movie, and we shot the scene. I knew that there was no way Jake Wild was even going to consider me so I pitched it to the moneymen behind Jake's back, managing to seal the deal with my "will-work-for-peanuts" offer. It worked. I'd once read that was how Nicole Kidman won the role in *To Die For*. She made a home movie to convince them—after they'd told her she was wrong for the part. Sometimes directors don't have faith in you and you have to prove yourself. Even if you're already a big star like me. In fact, sometimes even more so. Being a star (no pun intended) does have its problems—people think you're all celebrity and no talent. I had to show them they were wrong.

Janice was tidying up a pile of magazines and books. My face stared at me from two of the covers. It was always surreal seeing photos of myself and watching myself on screen. Like I was a totally different person. And I was.

"So why did Jake Wild ask you how you got the role? Doesn't he *know*?" Janice asked.

"Apparently not. I guess they never showed him my homemade film clip. He was so dead against hiring me from word go."

"And you think you convinced him at the read-through you're right for the part?"

"Maybe. But I think I've got to sweeten him up in other ways. Get him more on my side."

Janice raised a neat, shapely eyebrow. I'd been

trying my whole life to raise just one eyebrow and had never managed. "Seduce him?" Janice said warily.

I didn't answer. Just gave a little smirk. She knew me so well.

"That'll be easy, won't it?" she said. "Hasn't he fucked half of Hollywood? Like every single beautiful actress that he's ever met and worked with? I heard he slammed—who's that A-list actress with the big boobs and pouty lips?—I heard he fucked her in the elevator at the Golden Globes."

"Well, apparently—I heard this through the grapevine—he's not coming near me."

"Why the hell not?"

"Because *Skye's The Limit* is his big break and he doesn't want to 'screw with the talent.' "

"So fine. Leave him alone, then. Do your job and don't get involved. Isn't that better for you?"

"I have more control when they're lapping at my feet. You know, one time I didn't get along with my director. And guess what? I ended up on the cutting room floor."

"But they can't omit bits of the script and cut

your part short once you've started filming!"

"Oh yes they can. In that particular movie? This two-bit actress with three lines suddenly ended up being one of the most important elements of the storyline. Why? Because she was fucking the director and he was obsessed with her—" I took a swig of Diet Coke and went on— "Not that *I'm* fucking any of the directors— believe me—I mean, some of them are old enough to be my grandfather—but if that's the case I still sweeten them up so they're like father figures to me. Men either need to feel they have to protect me, or fuck me. And even if they're treating me like 'Daddy's little girl,' their secret fantasy is to have sex with me. They're men. That's how men think. Trust me, I've been working in this business since I was two years old."

"What about when you worked with that woman director—what was her name? *She* didn't want to fuck you."

"Maya? Well Maya was like a mother to me. With women it's easy. They're like your big sister or mom."

Janice plumped up the cushions around me

and folded up a cashmere wrap, laying it gently behind me. "Interesting theory."

"Except, oh yeah, when I was nine years old and shooting in Mexico? Before Mom died when she was in the hospital, and they gave me that lesbian freak as my chaperone, who I had to share a room with who, P.S., tried to freakin' rape me."

"Jesus, how awful! How come you never told me about her?"

"Because it's a memory I would rather bury. And you know what my agent asks before I sign? She makes sure there are no bull dykes because there is no way I'm working with some she-man who's going to try and get into my panties."

"But you kissed—no, *tongued*—what's-her-face—last year at the Grammy's? What's her name again, that singer?"

"She's a lipstick lesbian and I did it just for show. I was off my head, anyway. You know what the problem with Jake is? I don't know if he even finds me attractive."

Janice walked over to the window and looked out. "Of course he does—he'd have to be blind not to. Jesus, they're still out there. I can see one, like half a mile away, up in that tree at the Dufays' house. What *is* it with these paparazzi? Don't they have anything *better* to do with their time?"

"Well, when Jake looked at me the other day? He like *drilled* his eyes into me. It was scary. As if he was challenging me to a duel."

Janice turned around. "You find him sexy?"

"Well . . . I'm intimidated by him, although I'd never let him *know* that, of course. I respect him. And yes, he's drop-dead gorgeous with that husky British accent, not to mention his gorgeous body—of course I find him sexy—I'd be blind not to."

Janice smiled, knowingly.

"I don't think he's into me at all, though. I think he thinks I'm a spoiled, underage brat."

"You're over eighteen—you're not underage."

"I'm too young to drink legally."

"Well now you're *sober* that won't be a problem, will it, Star?" The 'will it Star?' was a glaring threat, Janice's sharp eyes locked onto mine and now she wasn't smiling.

I took a deep breath. "Look, this time I mean it. This time I have something to fight for."

"The part of Skye, you mean?"

"Exactly, I don't want to screw up. This is a once in a lifetime role. This could do for me what *Monster* did for Charlize or *Taxi Driver* did for Bobby. I cannot fuck my chances up." My cell started ringing and I stared at it. Very few people had my number. "Answer my phone, will you, Janice?"

She strolled over towards me and fished it out from under a cushion on the sofa. She looked at it and raised that eyebrow again. "Hello?" she said and then mouthed to me, 'Speak of the Devil'— "uh, I'm not sure if she's available right now—" there was a booming voice down the line that I couldn't decipher and then, "okay, okay, I'll put her on." Janice capped her hand over the mouthpiece and whispered, "He's pissed."

I took the phone gingerly from her hands. I looked at the screen. It was Jake. My stomach flipped. Why the hell was I getting butterflies when I thought he was such a jerk? "Yes?" I said coolly.

"Skye," he said.

"We're not on set yet, so you can call me Star."

"I'll get straight to the point. In your contract

it stipulates that the studio has the right to determine your accommodation for the duration of the shoot."

"Yeah?" I answered, wondering where this was leading. On location I'd stay wherever they had organized—we'd be in the Badlands for a while, and Mexico. I wasn't worried—I always ended up in amazing hotels with twenty-four hour room service. And now, with my home about to be remodeled, I thought a luxurious stint in The Four Seasons in Beverly Hills would be a great idea— better than a rental. The truth was, I'd spent my whole life in hotels and they felt more to me like home than my own house. No responsibilities. I *loved* hotels.

Jake's gravelly voice went on, "And they reserve the right to have any bodyguard of their choice, or any person deemed suitable, to offer you twenty-four hour security and vigilance." 'Vigilance' was a polite term for 'spying.' But still, it was that or nothing. I was hardly in a position to negotiate, so fresh out of rehab. There were other heavier, legal terms that went on for pages and pages in small print in the airtight contract I'd signed. I didn't bother reading it—I was so desperate to get the part of Skye that I didn't even go over it with my lawyer. She went ballistic, but with a list as long as my arm of all the A-list actresses vying for the part of Skye, there was no time to procrastinate.

"So they get to spy on me and have a bodyguard outside my door to make sure room service doesn't send me up a bottle of Stolichnaya . . . so . . . what's your point?"

"You're not staying at a hotel while your house is being remodeled, Star."

"Oh no? So where the hell am I going to stay? In a bed and breakfast? I've already taken a ridiculously low paycheck so they can damn well get me a decent hotel!"

"You'll be staying with me. At my house."

My mouth parted in shock.

"I don't like hotels," Jake explained. "I've got all my work gear at home so I'm not budging and the producers are insisting that I keep an eye on you. Basically, they want me to be your nanny. I won't lie, I've got better things to do with my time but . . . well, I don't seem to have much choice in the matter. Very unorthodox that's for sure. Why they couldn't just hire someone specific for the job, I have no idea."

"Obviously you're the only one they trust to do the 'job' properly because you have a vested interest in keeping me sober. However, Jake, if you've got so much to do, like you say, how will you have *time* to keep such an eagle eye on me? *Me*? Star Davis? who's been known to rappel out of windows in the dead of night by tying sheets together? who has bribed bodyguards and hotel cleaning staff to bring booze and drugs and even dancers and male strippers—"

"Exactly. Under my roof it'll be a little bit more tricky for you."

"Look, Mr. Clean. *Not*. I have no intention of screwing this up. So why don't you just give me a chance before assuming I'm a lost cause, okay?"

"I'll need you to be ready by Monday," he said, ignoring my little tirade. "Pack your stuff, and if you really want to make a fuss about it? Take it up with the studio, not me. What kind of food do you like?" he suddenly said, switching direction.

"I'm vegan."

"Great. Really easy-going, aren't you?"

"Do you know that nineteen thousand animals are slaughtered every MINUTE in the USA alone? and just because I don't want to be a part of this *evil*—knowing I'm swallowing a big mouth of suffering tortured pig that's been living in a concrete cell—where the poor creature can't even turn around—or eggs from chickens that live packed together with their beaks sawn off in their own stinking feces in a metal cage and—"

"I'm not judging you, Star, I'm sorry. Don't worry, I'll get my cook to sort something out. So what do you do about shoes, then, just out of interest?"

"Shoes?"

"Most shoes are made of leather."

"I wear Stella McCartney," I said quickly, remembering that I'd worn some Jimmy Choos to the run-through—a hundred percent leather. They were old ones—ones I'd bought before I turned completely vegan. But still. "Stella McCartney doesn't use any animal products in her collections," I added haughtily.

I could hear him smile through the telephone

line and it bugged me. He'd already caught me out.

LATER THAT DAY I went to see my new shrink. Well "shrink" is the wrong word because shrinks are able to prescribe medication and that was the last thing I needed: to get hooked on pills—any pills. People always assume drug addicts are going around with a needle stuck in their arm but no, most junkies are being aided and abetted by their very own doctors. Trust me, I know. My parents—Mom rest in peace—are great examples.

The truth is, I was very happy with my last therapist. He was cool. But in treatment, at rehab, it was decided by "the group" that I had been "manipulating" him, that he "had fallen into my trap" and that I was going nowhere fast if I continued on the same path. That's what happens in treatment. Your lies are exposed, your shell smashed so you are left with nothing but your own broken pieces, which you have to mend. The physical part of getting clean is nothing to what goes on mentally. Suddenly, you see yourself for who you are. I'm a work in progress—Jesus, I've only just begun—but I'm still not ready to let my barriers go completely. That's why I'm an actor. That's why I cling on to whatever role I have like a piece of driftwood in a raging sea. It's my only chance of survival. I need to hide behind another character. Because when I'm just me? I don't feel so great about myself.

But that's my secret. Even in rehab I tried my best to keep my walls from crumbling down. People don't like weakness. And who am I to disappoint them?

Back to my new shrink. She's a woman. I'll have to tell my whole story all over again and I'm yawning—yes yawning—when I say that. She's bound to feel sorry for me but I don't want sympathy. I've got two arms and two legs, and a job. I'm one of the lucky people and in the world and I don't take that lightly.

"SO WHERE DO YOUR PROBLEMS stem from, do you think?" Dr. Deal asked later. We were in her office and I was sitting comfortably in a big brown armchair, across from her desk, which was stacked with neat piles of paper—an old-fashioned fountain pen lay demurely on top of one pile. My hair was wet from a shower so I looked pretty drowned-rattish and she—well, she was immaculate in a Chanel-type suit (not *real* Chanel, obviously), and perfectly manicured nails which she held out in front of her, crisscrossed like show dogs sometimes do with their paws. She had smooth, shiny gray hair clipped into a page-boy cut and looked like she'd stepped out of an old copy of Vogue—or a collage of several old Vogues—because her hair and make-up was decidedly 1970s, but her suit was something from the 90s. A mixture of vintage—although perhaps that was accidental. Her mouth was a thin line—I could tell she was no-nonsense and her sense of humor on the back burner. Cool, ice-blue Nazi eyes. But there was a certain beauty about her. She must have been about fifty.

"Where do my problems stem from?" I

echoed. I learned this trick from them. To repeat the sentence. It made them question what they'd asked me. In their minds, anyway. "To be completely honest, Dr. De—"

"Please, call me Narissa."

"Narissa? That's a cool, unusual name." She didn't respond, her lip twitched into a wannabe smile but didn't quite get there. "Well, Narissa. I don't really see myself as having any problems at all. I've just landed a part in a movie that people would give their right arm for. I've got more money than people can even imagine earning in several lifetimes, a beautiful home, friends—you know, I'm really doing pretty darn well. But thank you for asking." I smiled sweetly at her.

"So why do you think you're here?"

"Why am I here? Because the studio believes that AA and NA are too public despite the fact that they promise anonymity."

"Narcotics Anonymous and Alcoholics Anonymous?"

I nodded. "Basically, it's in my contract that I come here. Plus, I wanted to show good will. To appease the studio, tow the line, and maybe, you know, talk about my addictive personality while

I'm at it."

"So you're willing to admit you have an addictive personality but you do not equate that with having 'problems' as such?"

"To me 'problems' are like, when you can't make payments on your home, or when you can't afford to feed your kids."

"Go on."

"I don't have any problems. Right now, I'm riding high."

She shifted in her chair and crossed her flesh-colored panty-hosed legs. "So you wouldn't consider that 'in denial' in any way?"

I shook my head. "I have nothing to deny. I'm honest."

"Why don't you tell me about your childhood, Star." This wasn't a question but a suggestion.

I inwardly rolled my eyes. *Uh, oh, here we go.*

She looked at her notes. "Your mother died of lung cancer when you were just ten years old. I'm so sorry for your loss."

"You've done your homework." She ignored my jibe.

"How did that make you feel?" she asked in a gentle voice.

"What do *you* think? I was only ten."

"Perhaps we can explore that. Were you angry? Did you feel abandoned?" *Right to the nitty-gritty, no beating about the bush, this one.*

"I don't know if you've ever watched someone die, uh, Narissa. But when a person is screaming in agony to 'just die goddam it, please just let me freaking die,' then you kind of pray that their suffering will end. So when it does, you're thankful. And when you miss them like crazy, two days later, because you realize they're not ever coming back, you wish that life wasn't so unfair and that it shouldn't have been that way. But it was, and there was nothing I could do about it."

"Those are very rational thoughts for a ten-year-old."

"What can I say? I was ten going on thirty."

"A grown-up mind in a child's body?"

"Exactly."

"How did the rest of your family take it?"

"You see, when you say the word 'family' I think of my co-stars. My family is whoever I'm working with at the time. Or better said, 'with whomever I'm working.' We become a unit. It's like, when you're doing a movie nothing else matters in the world, just the movie and the team making the movie. You become immersed in your work, in the minds and hearts of the other actors around you. The cameramen, Make-up, Hair, the electricians . . . everybody. You are one pulsing heartbeat."

"I was referring to your father. Your brother."

I could feel my insides coil at the word "brother." I felt sick, nauseous like I hadn't eaten all day. That empty yet bilious feeling, coming up like vomit. "My brother is not 'family.' And my father?" I could feel my sneakered foot tapping on the floor noiselessly. "Can we talk about this another day?"

"I see I've struck a nerve."

"I haven't even given my brother any mind-airtime for a long time. Because you know what? He's *out*. For. Ever. And my dad? When you've supported someone for as many years as I have? You get to be the parent and he gets to be the child. And that's what our relationship is, basically."

"Do you feel your dad—your parents—robbed you of your childhood? Starting working so young as you did?"

"Did they rob me of my childhood? I don't know. Because I can't compare my childhood to any other as it's the only one I've ever known. I can't tell you what it's like to stay at a school for more than nine months at a time because that was not my life. I can't tell you what it's like to experience first love, holding hands with a sweet-sixteen boy and making out at the back of a movie theatre. You know why? Because I *am* the movie theatre. I'm the spectacle. I'm the show."

"And how does that make you feel?"

I thought about it for a second and blurted out, "Lost. Powerful. Responsible. Hopeless. Elated. It depends on the day. The past is the past and I can't change a damn thing. The past shapes your present, your future."

"Would you change aspects of your childhood if you could go back in time?"

Jesus, she was like a machine gun and I was in her line of fire. Worse than a press junket! I looked up, my eyes straying to the left where I locked on a framed painting of a seascape done in oil. Perhaps it was there to make her patients—"clients"—feel at home. I'd once had an acting coach who said that people's eyes always went in the same direction every time they paused for thought. Up to the left, or right, or down to the floor. Or they leaned back in a chair or leaned forward, habitually doing the same thing, making the same motions, rarely changing their habits, and this defined their character. I was still looking up—to the left as it happened—and leaning back with no space between my back and the chair. This meant I was a "slow-time" personality, not "quick-time," or some such nonsense. Without looking at her I answered her question:

"I'd re-write the script, sure I would. I'd 86 my brother, I'd give my dad a leading role instead of the half-assed secondary character he played. I'd give my mom a happy ending—"

"Interesting that you see things in terms of 'roles.' And yourself?" she asked, her pale blue eyes drilling into mine—"what would you do for yourself?"

"I'm rewriting that part of the script right now. I'm taking control of my life."

"And the arrest prompted this one hundred and eighty degree shift in consciousness?"

"It did," I answered. "They—the State of California—forced me to go to rehab. Believe me,

I was kicking and screaming when I arrived at the clinic; it was not my idea of a vacation."

"So why don't you tell me about your arrest, Star?"

"Which one? There've been three. That one? The one I went to rehab for?"

"Whichever one you feel most comfortable discussing."

"None of them make me feel 'comfortable' exactly. I mean I'm not sinking into some feather bed here—no offense to you."

"Well why don't we talk about the time when you were arrested for disorderly conduct and violent behavior."

"Have you been Googling me?"

"Star, it's in both our interests to hear your side of the story. Your reasons, your motivation behind your actions. I can't help you if I don't know what you've been through. And yes, I *have* done my research, not to say that I hadn't heard about this on the news when it happened whenever it was last year."

"You want to know about the 'cat fight' then?"

"Is that how you would describe it, yourself? A cat fight?"

"That's what the papers said."

"And what do *you* say?"

"I was making a point. And I'm glad I got arrested, by the way. Not for all the other times because, hey, I was out of control drinking and driving and I could have done someone some damage, but the catfight? She deserved it."

"You don't think you could have made your point in a more controlled manner?"

"I was acting on impulse. She made me so mad, I had to *do* something."

"So you threw your drink all over her in the middle of an award ceremony?"

"It wasn't just any drink, it was a Bloody Mary, thick with tomato juice." My lips twitched into a subtle smile at the memory. "The red represented all the blood that had been spilled from innocent animals to create her tacky fur stole. There was a message."

"Lots of people wear fur. Surely you've seen women in fur walking down the street? What made you attack this particular woman in public?"

"Because they are not style icons getting paid twenty thousand dollars to get out of bed in the morning! She's one of the world's most famous supermodels and she's strutting around in *fur*? Think of all the young girls who think she's cool, who want to copy her style—" here I took a breath and realized how hypocritical I sounded . . . me, who'd passed out inebriated under tables in clubs, who'd been arrested for drunk driving, photographed with powder—white as a bunny rabbit's tail—all over my nose—and a thousand other things that young girls might think cool— "and, P.S.," I continued, "Miss Supermodel had done an anti-fur campaign, way back when at the beginning of her career. Did that not *mean* anything to her? Talk about hypocritical. No, you can berate me for many things I've done, but not that. Can we talk about something else? You know just thinking about it is making my blood boil."

I caught my therapist's eye. The "pity" look. "Go ahead," I said, "judge me with your steady eyes, but don't judge me on *that*." I took another long breath and felt my heart clatter inside my chest. I closed my lids to make the image of all the animal abuse in those PETA videos go away. People making money from death and suffering. *Ugh!* Spoiled rich bitches, trophy wives, swanning about in fur.

My therapist said softly, "I'm not judging you, Star. But maybe you judge yourself?"

I was used to this psycho-babble talk—trying to turn the tables on me. I took a sip of water. "Doesn't everyone judge themselves every day of the week? That little voice that says, 'Hey dummy, why did you do this or, why didn't you do that?' The Wouldda-Shoudda-Couldda voice? But I do my best within my boundaries. I have my morals."

"And they are?"

"Don't make money or seek pleasure from someone else's misery. And that includes all living creatures. Don't be disloyal to a friend. Don't steal. Don't hurt others—and yes, by drinking and driving I was potentially hurting others and that's why I've turned over a new leaf."

"Tell me about your addictions. Why do you do drugs and drink?"

Back to what a bad, bad girl I am. "*Did.* Not *do*. Past tense."

"Yes, I'm sorry. Why did you feel you needed to do drugs?"

"Why do people stuff their faces with too much food? Why do people tell lies? Maybe to protect themselves? To blot out insecurities,

57

drown out the white noise that hums in their brain? Who knows?"

"You used drugs as a way of blocking or numbing your thoughts?"

"When I get high, *got* high, it wasn't like a conscious, Hey I want to shut it all out, but more like, Hey, I wanna have some fun. You know? I'm nineteen years old. Can't a girl have some fun once in a while? It's hard being a grown-up all the time."

"You're alluding to your childhood? To the responsibilities you had as being the main breadwinner of the family?"

"The *only* breadwinner. Dad was my 'manager'. He 'managed' a lot of my money away, which wasn't the greatest when it came to paying my mom's medical bills, for instance. I bankrolled my brother's private school too: Groton. And the first two years of his college—"

"The first two years? He dropped out?"

"As soon as I got control back over my funds, last year, when I turned eighteen, I thought, Fuck *him*, why should I pay one cent more of his private education when the guy tried to ruin my life?"

"Tell me what happened between you and your brother."

"Another day perhaps. Suffice it to say that he and I are not exactly *close* and I'm glad I have bodyguards, you know what I'm saying?"

"He was abusive?"

"To put it mildly." My therapist nodded knowingly but her neat, silver bob stayed in place like a helmet.

"I'm sensing anger here, Star." She swiveled a sapphire ring on her middle finger so it was no longer lopsided. "We've touched on some important issues, obviously—things close to your heart."

"My brother is *not* close to my heart."

She nodded. And then said, "Do you feel you've been a victim of circumstance?" It was like she had pre-set questions—did she even care about my answers?

"My brother gets to be 'circumstance'?" I fired back at her. "No, there's no *circumstance* about it. Just Assholedom with a capital A."

"I understand that . . . you were a victim, I'm sorry."

I didn't like that word. Not at all. And I sure as hell didn't want her sympathy. "How can I be a 'victim' when I'm a movie star?"

"You say this as if you feel you have no right to feel vulnerable, or hurt, or damaged, as if only poor, less privileged people than yourself have the right to feel that way."

"Yeah, well, I guess the majority of people don't understand a poor-me attitude when it comes to the rich and famous."

"I think you need to give people more credit," she said. "Besides, everybody knows you give a lot of money to charity and that makes you popular. Your *Rising Star* school project for underprivileged girls? That's a very noble cause you set up, Star."

It was true that I'd spent a lot of my own money, and with help from Janice, we'd done a huge amount of fund-raising for the *Rising Star Foundation*. There were now eleven schools in five different countries, including the USA, and it was something I was really proud of. But I also knew from experience that people tended to focus on the negative.

"You know what the general public do?" I said. "Their eyes scan those cheap magazines at the supermarket checkout, and they gloat over celebrities' cellulite or zits, or the fact they've just broken up with their movie-star boyfriend. It's human nature. They don't have sympathy for us when we fall. Trust me. I've been around long enough to know."

"Yet you have nine million followers on Twitter."

"That means nothing."

"I think it means that you're extremely popular and your fans love you."

"It's not real love."

"And who would you say *does* love you, for real?"

I chewed the insides of my cheeks. Good question. Who actually loved me, apart from my oldest friend, Mindy? For *me*? Who I was? Janice? I was paying her so the line between employee and friend was kind of blurred. My dad? Did he love anyone but himself? In an insipid, pissy way, sure he loved me, but he'd hardly shown any real parental guidance or the kind of love that other people's parents demonstrated with their kids. He'd never suggested that I go to college, for instance, despite my aptitude for math and science. Jodi Foster—she'd gone to Yale even though she was a movie star. Emma Watson—the Harry Potter actress—Brown University, even when she was shooting practically back-to-back. It wasn't an impossibility. But it obviously hadn't occurred to Dad that I could do anything else with my life other than be in movies. Handy that—didn't want his resources to run dry.

"You don't seem to have an answer," said Narissa. Her eyes were as piercing as arrows in flight but her mouth now soft around the edges, tilting into sympathy. "Is that how you feel? 'Unloved'?"

I could feel an unwelcome lump in my throat, which I swallowed into a smile. "Sure people love me," I said, willing her off the subject with a flick of my wrist.

"Boyfriend?"

"I don't do boyfriends." My mind wandered to Jake and I wondered what it would be like to have someone like him as a boyfriend.

"But—"

"Oh, I guess you've read about that too. All my 'conquests' and all the guys I've dated. Don't you love that word 'date'? Like half the time you're not even *going* anywhere. Date is synonymous with 'fuck.'" I could see her wince at my choice of word as if she had a bad taste in her mouth.

Great—Miss Prissy as my shrink. That was all I needed. Or maybe she was *Mrs.* Prissy—perhaps she was married?

"So you've never had a serious relationship with a boy?" she pressed.

"What for? So they can go all *ego* on me and boss me around, or secretly film me with their iPhones and post it on YouTube and say what a slut I am?"

"Hopefully, if someone loved you you'd be able to build up a relationship based on trust, get to know somebody gradually without sexual relations at first."

"Yeah, well. I don't have time to get onboard *The Love Boat.* I go away too much. I never spend a whole night with anyone, you know? They never come to my house either. Too personal. Too risky. I always have my own wheels and leave the second I get bored or when the guy starts getting too lovey-dovey. I don't really *do* the intimacy thing."

"Hence your drunk/driving arrest?"

"Excuse me?"

"Driving when you shouldn't have. To make your getaway."

"I have a full-time chauffeur now. Just to be

sure. Look, I know what I did was wrong and believe me I paid for it. In every possible way. I had to do community ... hey, isn't our forty minutes up? Speaking of drivers, mine's outside waiting for me—I'm running real late." I stood up, gathered my purse and offered to shake her hand, which she reluctantly accepted. I guess she wasn't used to having her patients end the session first.

Narissa had wheedled more information out of me in one session than Larry—my old therapist— had done in six months. I had half a mind to fire her but a myriad of voices from rehab chirped in my ear. *Feeling uncomfortable, Star? Good! Now we're getting somewhere.* And, *"What doesn't break you makes you stronger."*

Most of the time I was sitting there, I had my mother on my mind—Mom's face a blur in my memory but my feelings never wavering—that physical ache I sensed inside me, remembering how she'd hold me and say, *You can do anything, baby, you know that?* And then her eyelids fluttering and her dozy smile as she nodded off from whatever downers she'd taken. Uppers to get her out of bed, yellow and turquoise, stripy or red.

Downers to calm her. When she was asleep I'd line them up, color-coordinated or in heart shapes or zigzag patterns. Once I popped one in my mouth thinking it would taste like candy but quickly spat it out; cruel and bitter. At the time I didn't understand why she'd want to eat something that didn't taste good.

My mom had always believed in me. When we had no money and lived in a trailer, she'd spend her last dime on a pretty dress for me, or gas for her old spluttery Oldsmobile to get me to an audition on time. Even if she relied on her "mother's little helpers" to get her through the day, she never once was late, hauling me off to meet a director, or us standing in line for some open cattle call where I'd have to sing and dance, or show them my tap dancing skills. Toothy-gum smile. Little knock knees. Long blond hair to my waist. Smiling and happy, even if I preferred to be playing soldiers with my brother or Doctors and Nurses in the trailer park with Mindy. No video games—we couldn't afford them. We lived from commercial to commercial and it wasn't until I was seven and got my first TV show that the money started properly rolling in.

I wanted to please my mom—make her proud. And now I had that same feeling about Jake and I didn't understand why. It wasn't just the movie I cared about or doing a good job, but Jake himself. I was yearning to impress him. And at the same time, the Machiavellian devil in me was urging me to play little power games—just to see if I could get to him.

I decided that staying with him in his house . . . Would be a whole lot of fun.

"SO THIS IS FOR REAL?" Mindy said, and then she slurped up her strawberry, wheat-germ and banana smoothie through a straw even though there was nothing left at the bottom. Her round, apple cheeks always gave her an air of happiness, and her sparkly brown eyes—like the cutest puppy ever—made me feel that the world was right even when it wasn't. She always complained about being overweight but she had one of the most beautiful faces I had ever seen, like an innocent angel from a Renaissance painting. Timeless beauty. I felt safe with her and one hundred percent accepted. We went back a long way Mindy and I, and she'd seen the worst of me but had still hung around all those years—never letting me down even when I'd been an ass. One of the few people I could trust because we'd known each other since we were four. When you're famous you can never be sure who your real friends are—some people can do a very convincing act.

We'd been shopping and were now hanging out on Santa Monica Pier, people-watching—at least trying to. For me it wasn't so easy. I was wearing a huge purple hat, dark sunglasses—my signature long blond hair tucked inside a belted mackintosh that made me look like some detective from a pulp fiction crime novel. Except the hat was one of those oversized floppy ones so maybe I looked like something out of a 1980's Jackie Collins 'bonkbuster'—the kind my mom used to read. So far, only two people had recognized me but I kept my head down and kept on walking— no eye contact. One of my bodyguards walked ahead of us and another behind. Things had calmed way down since my arrest and three-night stint in jail, but having swarms of paparazzi trailing me could be terrifying and I didn't want to get caught unawares.

"He doesn't want me to stay with him but the producers are insisting," I told Mindy.

"What about Janice, is she coming too?"

"Good point. I guess not. I'll need her though so maybe I should bring her along."

"No, no distractions," Mindy said emphatically. "Jake Wild is a serial womanizer. He might be attracted to her."

"Over *me*?"

"You already said he wants to stay clear of you so yeah, he might go for Janice."

"Yeah, we can't have that."

"Guys go crazy when women fool around with them and then don't give a damn. Makes them nuts!" She grinned at me. "Serves them right most of the time—gives them a taste of their own medicine." That was my signature behavior with guys. . . Treat 'em mean, keep 'em keen and Mindy lived vicariously through me. She'd had her heart broken once and since then hadn't dared trust a guy. If I treated someone badly it gave her a thrill as if her ex was getting direct punishment. "All men are the same," she added. "Serves 'em right to get their butts kicked once in a while."

My gaze wandered to the horizon where a sailboat was dipping into a golden sun—it reminded me of a painting by William Turner; the light luminescent, flickering and changing hue by the second. Like me. Changeable. Mercurial. Running from one role to the next; the real 'me' always in question.

"Yeah," I said distractedly. "But Jake's a determined type, stubborn—you can see it in his jaw, you know the kind? Daddy issues. Wants to prove himself."

Mindy laughed. "How d'you know that?"

"Google."

"His daddy issues are common *knowledge*?"

"No, but I can read between the lines. Takes one to know one."

"Jake's dad's a producer, right? And his uncle won all those Oscars for Best Director and for that movie Angelina Jolie was in? What was it called? That was his last big hit?"

"Daddy's a powerful player in this town. Real

asshole. Ruthless and tough. Bet he beat the shit out of Jake when he was a boy."

"You've done too many years of therapy, my dear. I'm sure Jake was just *fine* and had a golden, blessed childhood with all that cash floating around."

"No, he isn't fine. I can read his eyes. He has a *wild*, feral look about him, like he could do anything, like he has a secret temper. Like he could go off the rails."

"Well if anyone can test him, it'll be you." She looked at me to gauge my expression and added seriously, "He's fucked around a lot so be on your guard." Mindy winked at me and I smiled wanly, feeling the emptiness at the pit of my stomach. Flirting and fooling around with guys was second nature. The truth was that every single make-out episode was a blank. I guessed it was more about control than pleasure. I'd save the love crap for a rainy day. Meanwhile, Jake could eat his heart out. How dare he think that he could resist me? Not only was I going to show him I could act, I'd have him right where I needed him:

Under my thumb.

PRODUCTION
Shooting Star

DIRECTOR
Jake Wild

DATE
May

SCENE
Leo and Jake

TAKE
6

CAMERA
Jake Wild

"**F**UCK YOU'RE TALENTED," Leo said as he thumbed his way through my storyboards for *Skye's The Limit*. "No, really, is amazing."

Leo was Ukrainian—hence the thick accent and absence of articles in his speech, although his vocabulary was pretty impressive. He'd become a close buddy of mine during the last six months and was going to be my AD—assistant director—for the shoot. He was the same age as me and I'd found him fresh out of the London International Film School. I'd set up a competition for a ten-minute short and his was—amongst an ocean of talent—my favorite work. He'd done a sort of collage; half animated, half with actors—the subconscious mind and dreams of a man in turmoil. I loved Leo's arty style and saw a great future for him so signed him up to work for me.

He was looking at the storyboards for the car chase scene in the Badlands I was mapping out. "Is incredible how you plan ahead. Me? I just go with flow, you know? Make it up as I go along. They call me pantster in USA, like I'm driving by seat of pants." He slapped me on the back, laughed and drained his glass. "Mind if I give myself top up?"

"Feel free," I said, watching his tall frame bound up from the sofa and swagger purposefully toward the drinks' cabinet, the bangs of his thick dark hair obscuring his face. He was thick set, handsome and very muscular—his myriad tattoos making him look rough and tough—I noticed that women went crazy for him, partly because of his unnerving charm and brazen confidence.

"So when's girl arriving?" He filled up his glass with vodka and clunked in a few ice cubes.

"Today," I said.

"Very sexy girl. Very hot," he suggested meaningfully, with a vigorous nodding of the head. Leo and I had done our fair share of partying together. We made a good team—pretty wild when we got going. He had a penchant for curvy women, in particular.

"I'm not going there, Leo," I warned.

"Why fuck not? Come with job, no? Like Parmesan on pasta or vodka with caviar. You can't have one without other."

"Not this time. I need to concentrate. Besides, she's too young. Practically underage. The last thing I want is to break her heart. Especially when we have a film to do together. I can't have her crying on me, or worse, using drugs again. Or getting drunk and maudlin."

I didn't want to sound arrogant but it was true. For whatever strange reason, women ended up falling in love with me—at least that's what they told themselves—how genuine it was, I very much doubted. But still, it was always a downer in the end. I was out to have some fun (making it clear from the start that there were no strings attached) and the next thing I knew they were planning some phantom honeymoon.

"Ha!" said Leo, letting out another chuckle, "bet you concentrate on tits and ass—not if she gets her lines right, no?"

Just then there was a huge commotion—my dog barking at the back door where deliveries arrived. Biff—my assistant—rushed in, her arms thrown up in the air in defeat. Her name "Biff" said it all. She was chunky—a boxy body with no waist—her jeans slung low like a rapper, keys dangling from her belt. Her brown hair was cropped short and she habitually wore sneakers, huge, baggy black T-shirts, no make-up and never any perfume. I liked her that way, e.g. no temptation. I'd ended up fucking every single one of my assistants up until Biff and it had always ended in tears. They'd wanted more than just to work for me. This way I couldn't cross the barrier. Besides, I was pretty sure that Biff was a hundred percent gay.

"I'm so sorry, Jake," she said in her deep voice, "I totally forgot to mention her chef was delivering stuff ahead of time."

"Whose chef?"

"Star Davis's. He's at the door. He's bringing her weeks' supply of food. Fresh and frozen stuff for her mini-meals. She eats several mini-meals a day, like J-Lo—at least that's what I read in National Enquirer. Or maybe it was somewhere else I read—"

"What the fuck? I told her my cook would sort something out!"

"From what I've read, this chef is 'haute cuisine vegan' if that makes sense. Used to work for Madonna."

Leo was holding his sides, laughing. "She's going to be bundle of fun, this one."

Star Davis taking over my life already and she hadn't even arrived yet. "Fine. Just go and deal with it, Biff. Show him around the kitchen. Offer him a drink or a cup of tea. Is there anyone else I should be expecting? Any other of Star's entourage?"

Biff nibbled her lower lip. "Well her masseuse will be coming by three mornings a week. And her personal trainer every day, except Sunday. Her acting coach and, um, I think that's it. Oh, and also her hairdresser called to say he'd be by on

Tuesday. Oh yes, and her bedding."

"What?" I yelled.

"She has a bed and special mattress that's being delivered too. Made of cashmere or something. Same thing Princess Anne has. I read these swanky mattresses cost up to fifty-five thousand dollars—custom made, hand crafted, used by the Savoy Hotel in London for their presidential suites."

"Are you serious? A fucking *bed* is being delivered to my house?"

"And special sheets and pillows and so on. Zillion count Egyptian cotton." Biff made a face as if to say, *Well, it is Star Davis*—and rushed out of the living room.

Leo was grinning. "Don't look so gloomy, Jake. You get to try out cashmere mattress. Test for quality. Test talent. Ha, ha."

"I will *not* be fooling around on that mattress, Leo, I can guarantee you."

"If you don't want to sample goods, then I will—" He stopped dead in his tracks, his mouth gaping open. I turned around and saw Star walk coolly into the room as if she owned the place.

"Hi guys. I'm early. Just thought I'd make a few arrangements—you know, make myself at home, hope you don't mind."

Leo's eyes slid down Star's body—from where he was standing across the room—around her pert but ample cleavage, down to her nipped in waist, the tight little skirt, down her long, smooth, golden legs and back up to her face, resting on her pouty lips and then trailing up to her big blue eyes. My heart was beating but I did no more than steal her a glance—I didn't want to indulge her ego. My eyes were on Leo as he stripped her naked. But she wasn't his usual type! A surge of inexplicable jealousy ripped through me. I stared at him, shaking my head with a silent warning: *No you fucking don't, mate.*

"**L**EAVE, LEO," Jake barked as I entered his living room for the first time. As I stood there, thrilled confusion spiked my veins. Not one, but two hot men both turned their heads to stare at me: Jake, and this guy named Leo.

Jake said, "I mean it, Leo. We'll talk later, okay?" His voice was no-nonsense—a man used to bossing people around. "I need to clear up a few things with Star, first. Excuse my manners; Leo, this is Star, Star Leo. He's my AD."

"Attention Disorder?" I said with a hint of a smile.

Leo enjoyed my joke and sauntered toward me

slowly, undressing me with his deliciously wicked eyes. He had "bad boy" written all over him. I knew the type. The kind I'd try to drink under the table (failing) or play roulette with (winning). The type that would definitely drive a car too fast. Know where to get the best drugs. Who'd try to slam you up against a wall rather than take you to bed. He was tall, taller than Jake—and very muscly. He had YOU'RE MINE stamped on his forehead, dancing in his intense green eyes. His hair was dark, mussed up. I knew I had to keep myself well away from him. A party boy if ever I saw one.

He took my hand and kissed it but pulled me towards him, gripping my fingers somewhat, leaning in close and said—his accent was foreign, Russian or something—and laced with innuendo, "We'll be seeing each other, Star. Oh yeah." He winked at me and smirked a little like he'd already had his way with me.

"No," I said. "I doubt I'll be seeing you but you *will* be seeing *me*—through your camera lens." I tossed my head cockily.

But he ignored my quip and whispered in my

ear, "How loud?"

I crunched my brows at him. "What?"

He lowered his voice almost inaudibly so Jake couldn't hear, "How loud will you scream when I fuck you?"

My mouth hung open. He didn't even know me! But his arrogance was amusing—I had to admit. I was about to slap him across the face (just for good measure) but he turned on his heel and was out the door in a flash.

Jake's gaze penetrated me. "What did he say to you?"

I shrugged. "None of your business."

"Well it is kind of my business, actually. You're my property, Star—at least for a while."

His words excited me for some reason; I liked the idea of him feeling possessive over me but I retorted, "Me? Your property? In your dreams, Mr. Director."

Jake added, "Leo really fucks around, you know. Watch out."

"So do I."

Jake squinted his eyes, challenging me.

"Anyway, you're one to talk," I shot back,

knowing his reputation as a major womanizer.

"I don't want you getting distracted during filming."

"Hang on a minute! Not wanting me to drink and do drugs is one thing but you can't control who I hang out with. Or date!"

"Just watch me, Star."

"What, you're going to lock me in a room, or something?"

"I won't have to—you're not going anywhere fast."

"Oh no? What makes you so sure?"

"Your bed"—a flicker of a smile. At first I thought he was suggesting something but then it dawned on me. My bed was here—I hated sleeping on strange mattresses and he knew I had no intention of going anywhere. Caught out. Again.

Jake walked slowly toward me. He stood there, legs astride. Assertive. Strong. I could smell him; sun, and a woody, masculine aroma that I couldn't place that brought back some happy memory buried deep within me. Jake took my hand in his and grazed his fingers over my knuckles. This tiny gesture of affection shot a bolt of desire through my limbs to my core—a shudder that caused goose pimples to break out all over me.

"You're special, Star—so beau—" he stopped mid-sentence—"don't misdirect your energy. I want you to concentrate on your part. This movie's your chance, don't blow it. Anyway, I've got to go to a meeting now. Big John's outside, watching the house, so don't try anything funny. I won't say 'make yourself at home' because you already have. I'll be back in a few hours."

I watched him walk calmly out the door, purposefully on his way to whatever meeting he had.

All he cared about was the movie.

PRODUCTION
Shooting Star

DIRECTOR
Jake Wild

DATE
May

SCENE
Sex Addicts Anon

TAKE
8

CAMERA
Jake Wild

THIS WAS THE PART I fucking hated. Sitting around in a circle, feeling self-conscious and having to bloody "share." So far, I'd managed to avoid it but this was my sixth meeting so people were beginning to eye me up with expectation. I took a breath and said, "Hi, my name's Jason and I'm a sex addict." I cringed at my words—still didn't quite believe them. But here I was—proof that I had to turn my life around for the better.

"Hi Jason, so glad to have you here," said an old hippy type with round glasses and stringy gray hair. Not the sort of person I had imagined being here, but of course being a sex addict isn't really about sex; it goes deeper than that.

"Hi Jason," several people mumbled, smiling hopefully.

"I . . . um . . . well, I just thought I'd say that I've been abstinent for two weeks and—" I paused, wondering what the fuck I should tell them. That I was climbing the walls? That giving up sex was a thousand times worse than not drinking, not smoking, not taking drugs, all rolled into one? That having Star in my house was like having the Devil as your best mate, when you were training to take your vows as a priest? "Well, hello everyone," I concluded awkwardly, feeling like a prize jerk.

A gangly woman who must have been about thirty said, "Thank you for sharing." And then everyone chanted in unison, "It works if you work it. Thank you for sharing." I looked at them and then back at her and thought how incongruous she looked in this setting. You'd think sex addicts would be sexy. But people looked "normal"— boring, really—and definitely not sexy. Luckily.

The last thing I needed was more temptation. We weren't in the more glamorous West Hollywood branch, no. I wasn't that stupid. I knew that most of that sex addict lot went purposefully to hook up, and to the AA and NA meetings specifically to do movie deals. I was anonymous here in the Valley. Or so I hoped.

I wasn't lying when I said my name was Jason—it *is* my real name but nobody calls me that except my mother and a few old friends. SAA— Sex Addicts Anonymous or, as some call it, SLAA, Sex and Love Addicts Anonymous. But "love" wasn't my problem. I'd never been in love. Love didn't come into it. It was like being a wild cat hunting for prey and women were my dinner. If I saw a pretty woman somehow it felt wrong not to make a play for her. I needed a weekly conquest— sometimes even daily—to keep myself functioning. Sex was my drug. No prostitutes. No excessive porn. No—I wanted the real thing, not some fake image on a screen and I sure as hell never needed to pay for it. It was easy for me. Stunning women were at my beck and call. Perks of being a movie director. I was rich. Most people described me as good looking. Sex for me was like brushing my teeth—something that was necessary. Easy.

Often I wondered what it was, exactly, that gave me my high. I think it was the intensity. The adrenaline of the chase. And the thrill of having someone so into me. Yeah, yeah, my shitty childhood didn't help my self-esteem issues. Been there, done that. Done the whole shrink thing, the mother abandonment issues, the father-beat-the-shit-out-of-me saga, the little boy sexually abused at boarding school. The lonely lost boy who needed love and affection, seeking it the only way he knew how: through sex.

But the bottom line was—for whatever bullshit reason—here I was, needing more.

More, more, *more.*

It was as if my dick had a brain of its own. Not a very intellectual one (no kidding) but a force that propelled me to do things, even when logically I knew it was crazy. Fucking women in public places, having pretty women I "needed" flown out to me on private jets while I was on location, just to get my fix—the list went on and the bills piled up. Dinners, transport, jewelry, cars. I may have been a "love-em-and-leave-em" bastard but I was a generous one. But it got to the point that it was affecting my career—compromising my work by hiring actresses for their fuckability, not their talent.

Being an addict is expensive. You're ruled by a more powerful force and you're out of control. You convince yourself you're calling the shots but no, it's your cock. Dick has you as his slave, his minion, dancing to his horny tune that blares in your ears twenty-four seven.

And each time I—the lion—caught his catch, I always found myself plummeting to a low like a come-down after drugs, and the only thing that would set me right again was seeking a new thrill—jumping back on the roller coaster, all over again. Over and over. And now I was fucking burnt out.

I'd pushed myself to my limit and had to stop.

And then I met Star bloody Davis.

And all I could think of since I first set eyes on her—twenty-four hours a day—was when, and how, I'd fuck her.

9
Star

STAYING IN JAKE'S HOUSE was less fun
than I had imagined. The big wild partygoer
licking coke off nubile starlets' navels, two at a
time? Dancing on tables? Not a bit of it. He was
quiet and reserved. Brooding even. Most of the
time he was talking on the phone or working on
his laptop—completely ignoring me. Yet if I
strayed toward the front door—his eyes on his
work—it was as if he had a sixth sense. "Where-
the-fuck-d'you think you're going?" he'd say
without looking at me. It didn't matter what I
did—walk round half naked in a skimpy bikini, not
wear a bra, sit with my legs wide apart so he could

see right through my panties (*if* he'd paid attention)—or even "accidentally" bump into him when I was naked after a shower—he'd brush past me as if I were a slightly irritating little sister or something.

Sure, I had the run of the house and he was treating me well in that way—my own suite, with a huge bedroom and a beautiful view to the pool area, where lemon trees, lush palms and tropical green foliage spilled onto a mossy lawn. It was like a wall of vegetation—very private, no neighbors could see in—which suited me perfectly. So far, I'd out foxed the paparazzi. At least, there wasn't the usual crowd of them hovering around. But the place was eerily silent except for maybe music or the tweeting of birds, or the mumble of Jake's voice as he made his pre-production calls to his crew or producers.

I was lonely.

His house was grand; enormous, with polished Spanish tiled floors stretching across huge, echoey hallways. I took to going barefoot so my shoes wouldn't make clicking sounds. There were elegant arched windows, a sweeping staircase, and oil paintings looming big on every wall. One was of a beautiful 1920s flapper with cropped black hair, holding a cigarette in a silver holder, and looked like an original Tamara Lempicka. In the garage behind the house were not just one, but two, classic cars: an old silver Rolls Royce from the 1950s and a navy blue Bugatti sports car. Jake had opulent but unusual taste.

With nothing to do but learn my lines, I made friends with Jake's dog, a huge Rhodesian Ridgeback with golden eyes and, like his namesake, he had a permanent ridge of hackles that stuck up along his backbone. His name was Fierce but he was a sweetheart and we quickly became close.

Jake ignored members of my staff as they came and went: my masseuse, my chef, my hairdresser, who passed by to touch up my highlights. Jake was polite but reserved. Never once did he berate me for having so many people invading his home, and for the first time I became self-conscious—aware that having a team fluttering about me wasn't really normal; not the way most people lived. Jake had money but he didn't seem to need an entourage to support him, to cater to his every whim. I had indulged myself too much and now it was beginning to dawn on me that privacy—having moments completely to myself with just the dog, for instance—was actually a good thing.

There was a magical peace in Jake's house that I hadn't experienced before. A calming experience. Jake was there physically but also benignly absent—an old married couple who no longer spoke to each other—that's what it felt like between us. At least to me. I still couldn't work out what his game plan was—if he had one. Every so often, I'd catch him observing me. A flicker of a second, a dart of the eyes, but then he'd go back to pretending I hardly existed.

The more he ignored me, the more I wanted his attention.

After a couple days of this (we were about to start filming in two days' time) Jake finally broke the silence.

"You know all your lines or just the first few scenes?" he asked out of the blue.

"I always like to learn the whole script so I know it backwards."

"Good girl."

"I'm not a girl, I'm a woman, if you hadn't noticed." But when he said "good girl" my heart skipped a beat. He had just come out of the pool, trailing water as he walked into the living room, and his dirty blond hair was slicked back wet, a white towel carelessly slung about his hips, accentuating that manly V, his body bronzed—and for the first time I got to see how beautiful the contours of his muscles were: his arms taut and strong, his chest wide, narrowing beautifully down to a segmented stomach. Not bulky or thick—but lean like a tennis or soccer player—somebody muscular because of sport, not because of weights. It was the first time he'd had a swim since I'd been here—usually he was in the main living room, his head buried in a huge great art book, gleaning inspiration for a scene or watching old movies with the blinds drawn, freeze-framing and snapping a shot with his iPhone or sketching a new idea for his storyboards. Then he'd be on the phone forever, talking to producers or location managers, or with Leo about the shooting schedule, changing things up at the last minute.

Pre-production details. Cool, calm, on top of things.

In this instant I had him to myself, as I drank in his body, admiring him the way you might a Greek marble statue at the Met or some Italian fountain in Rome.

"I like to be flexible," he told me, his eyes flickering for just a millisecond to my breasts before he settled back on my eyes. Water was dripping from his body like raindrop crystals. Everything seemed in slow motion—freeze-framed for me as I blinked like a camera lens to take in the shot—to save the image for later. I swear I could feel the electricity charging between us but then he looked away (upward to the right, funnily enough) squinting his gray eyes in thought, and I understood it was my imagination that had had him wanting me, desiring me. Because never had a guy ignored my come-ons so much as Jake. Never. My nipples were poking through a see-though top—I too had been swimming earlier, my hair still damp—and the air conditioning in the room had chilled them into little peaks. All for nothing! I could have been a chair or a table as far as he was concerned—so little did I matter to him, except as a tool for his movie.

"I thought we could do a few acting exercises," he said. "Not the scenes themselves but a bit of improvisation."

I loved improv. Some indie directors did whole films by way of improvisation; practically ignoring the script or making it up it as they went along—letting their actors come up with ideas to shape the scenes.

Jake wasn't looking at me when he asked, "You're into the Method, I hear?"

I nodded. "It's the only way I know how to work—to get into character. Except I can't exactly go around *killing* people so I guess for *Skye's The Limit* I'll have to actually *act* and forget the Method." I thought he'd laugh but he didn't.

"There's the sex scene," he said, choosing his words carefully, "and I don't know how we should go about shooting it. I've been worrying about it for days. Have you got any ideas, Star? Of Skye's motivation in this scene?"

"It's all about control," I answered. Skye and I were so similar in many ways—I really identified with this part. "She wants to get her way so she's using sex as a weapon."

"You see, I don't see it as black and white as that. I think she's yearning for attention—to be loved. A need for love is driving this scene, not control. She's using sex as a way to get close to men, as it's the only way she knows. I think this scene is pivotal; its when the audience needs to realize how alone she is. It's imperative that the audience fall in love with her at this point." He looked up and his penetrating eyes locked with mine. I felt myself tingle all over. But I also wondered if there was some message—a personal one for me—buried in his words.

"You look cold, Star. I'll turn off the air con." As he said this, his eyes ran down to my breasts again. Double messages, dammit. Then he walked over to the wall switch and flicked off the air con, meanwhile dimming the lights. A beam of late afternoon sunlight shot through a crack in the blinds leaving a golden ray across the dark wooden floor but apart from that we were in semi darkness. I was hoping he'd want to enact the scene from the movie with me, when I seduce the prison guard.

"Shall we do that scene?" I asked eagerly, "when I kiss the—"

"No kissing, Star. Just . . . let's pretend you want to dance with me—you can take this scene in any direction you want; it doesn't have to be dancing—that's just an idea. But you need to persuade me—get my attention." He sat down in a chair and picked up a book, ignoring me the way he had for the past few days. *Get his attention?* So far it had been impossible and I'd been working on it, practically around the clock.

How could I break him down this time? *Get* to him? My iPod was lying on the coffee table atop a pile of art and film books. I picked it up, scrolled through my playlist and chose "Drunk in Love" by Beyoncé. I padded over to him in my bare feet and stood before him. *Nothing.* No reaction. I began to swing my hips in time to the music, hovering my ass over his lap—yeah, I'd do a lap dance just for him. In my previous movie I'd played a stripper who had a child to support and a mom with Alzheimer's—my character desperately needed the money. I'd trained enough to know what I was doing—spent weeks learning to pole dance. I was good.

I began to gyrate slowly, leaning in on him, with my ass brushing past his stomach. Did I feel a hard rod dig into me as I eased my butt in little circles? Or was it my imagination again? I bent down so he could get the full peachy view, my short skirt edging higher up my thighs so he could see my panties. I was moist down there—turned on by our proximity. I could hear his heavy breaths and he grabbed my hips. Hard. His fingers digging into my flesh, his grip firm, his thumbs pushing into each cheek as he steadied me so I couldn't move an inch. His touch shot shivers down my spine—goose bumps crept all over me. I could feel myself moisten up even more. His hold on me was dominating. Raw.

"No, Star." His grip was relentless. The music continued but I couldn't move.

"What's wrong?"

"I asked you to get me to dance with you."

"I *am* dancing with you."

"You're dancing *at* me. I need to want to participate."

My back was still to him—he couldn't see, thank God—the tears of humiliation welling in my eyes. Rejection. Being spurned. "What do you want?" I whispered.

There was a long pause and he said, "You need to break me. Not sexually but in a deeper more metaphysical way."

Metaphysical? WTF? "Oh."

"What's the action in this scene?"

"To cry?" *That would be easy at this point.*

"That could be the result. What's the *action*?"

The lump in my throat hardly let me say the words, "I don't understand you."

"The action that's driving this scene? What does Skye want?"

"She wants to get the hell out of jail!"

"And what's stopping her?"

"The prison guard." *Duh!* "He's her last hurdle. He's the only thing stopping her freedom." *You know that, you jerk!*

"This guard is being played by a fifty-year-old. And remember this is set in 1964 and things were different then. You'll have to think of a better way to 'seduce' him because if you do it like this—so blatantly—the audience will not only lose respect for Skye, they'll be turned off."

Jake was turned off. *He* had lost respect for me. This playing-out-a-scene game before official rehearsals was *bullshit* and I'd had enough.

"Let me go, you asshole!" I cried out, freeing myself from his grasp. "You've been screwing with my head for days. Ignoring me. Making me feel small and worthless like I'm invisible! You're worse than my father. Using me for your own ends. Not even thinking for one moment that I'm only nineteen and just because I look like a woman on the outside and grew up before my time—" The words flew out of my mouth surprising even me—"I'm . . . I'm . . . People just want me for what I can offer them: money, a performance for their movies—it fucking *sucks*!"

He spun me around so I was facing him. A glow of warmth flickered in his eyes, and his lips lifted into an almost imperceptible smirk as if he'd won a prize. But then he frowned. He looked up at me and he said, "Bring that vulnerability to this scene, Star."

"What? Are you *serious*? I am not *acting* right

now! This is for real, Jake. I feel used, like you just don't give a shit about me as a person." I struggled from his grip but he pulled me close so my crotch was practically in his face—he was still sitting. He bit his lower lip, lust oozing from his pores like rising steam. My eyes dropped down. His swim shorts were tented. He was huge. Hard as a rock. So I *did* affect him after all—my little dance had turned him on! But he suddenly let me go and stood up abruptly, turning his back on me.

"Coward," I spat out at his strong golden shoulders.

"Fighting your demons head on is *not* cowardly, you should know that by now."

I stared at the back of him, imagining myself tussling his hair, grabbing it as he pinned me on the sofa. I wanted him to kiss me, shut the words coming out of his mouth with my mouth.

"You don't know me, Star. Just think of me as your director, nothing more. The only thing I'm good for, as far as you're concerned, is getting a great performance out of you. Trust me—I'm bad for you on any other level."

"Can't we at least be friends?" my voice

croaked.

He jerked around and looked me hard in the eye. "Honestly? I doubt that very much."

His words were like daggers. "Why do you dislike me?"

"Dislike you? Is that what you think?" He shook his head. "Come here, Star. Let's sit down and talk, this is crazy."

I slumped down on to the oversized couch, sinking into its feathery comfort, watching him watch me. Boy, was he a mind fuck, or what.

"Hang on," he said, "I'll get us some drinks."

There was a liquor cabinet hidden in a bookshelf, which I'd had no idea about. The hinges were so small when it swung open, revealing a mindboggling array of bottles—like something out of a Bond movie. Jake poured a couple of Cokes, clinked in some ice and slices of lemon. I tucked my knees under me and wondered what he wanted to talk about. My character, Skye, no doubt. Jake—a one-track mind: the Movie, with a capital M.

He sat down, close enough, but making sure he wasn't touching any part of my body. His erection had calmed down and I had that niggling question again; had I imagined it? He had his "I'm a Director" look on again.

"Look," he began.

"I'm looking," I retorted childishly. "And I can't see the freaking wood from the trees. You're giving me double messages, Jake. You think I want to be here as your prisoner? I could be in a hotel with my friends having fun, not alone here where the only person—I mean creature—that pays any attention to me is your dog!"

"I don't know how to deal with you." He took a long slug of his soda. Was he abstaining from booze for my sake? "You're disarming me. I'm trying to be professional and I'm finding it extremely difficult the way you're . . . you're . . . look . . I don't want to hurt you."

"Ha! They warned me that you were a player but nobody filled me in about your arrogance. Hurt me? Star Davis? I don't fall in love, Jake. Least of all with directors."

"Then why are you acting all wounded when I don't pay you more attention?"

He had a point. "I . . . I don't know what you're talking about."

"This business is a lonely, dog-eat-dog one, and people are out for your blood. I'm just trying to protect you, Star. Like you pointed out earlier, you're only nineteen."

"Oh yeah? Like you're not *one* of them? You want my blood just as much as the next person. Last I heard, all you cared about was getting a great performance out of me and that there's no way we can be friends!"

"You think we can be buddies when you run around in tiny little skirts—your exposed legs all long and golden, your sexy little arse cheeks peeking out all over the place? Oh, and naked as well! With your beautiful tits in my face? Don't you get it, Star? *Course* I want to fuck you! Any straight man would. All day long, all I think about is sex. With you. But we simply can't go there!"

I felt my stomach flip with triumph. Excitement. I'd *got* to him! I felt powerful. Like holding a great hand of cards, I knew I could win this game. "I'm sorry," I said, putting my hand lightly on his thigh. I could hear the pattern of his breath was uneven and when my eyes strayed to his newly tented shorts—that comforting telltale sign—it sent a tingle between my legs. He desired me. And his desire was turning me on.

"We need to talk—get to know each other a bit better. I'm sorry I haven't handled things so well, it's just . . . I find you disconcerting."

"Disconcerting?" I played the innocent.

Then he said between gritted teeth, "Do you always get what you want, Star?"

"*You're* a person who gets what he wants," I answered, "you should understand. But there's one difference between us: I had to *fight* for my privileges but you were born with a silver spoon in your mouth."

He laughed. "The spoon was pretty bloody tarnished, I can tell you."

"Oh, yeah. Your dad's one of the richest producers this side of Hollywood, and your uncle and grandfather are Academy Award winning directors with a list as long as my arm of hit movies. Tough life, Jake Wild."

He shook his head, an ironic smile tilting up his lips. "It wasn't all roses I can tell you."

It was true. Who was I to decide who he was? I hardly knew the guy, except what I'd read in the papers or heard about through friends. "What about your mom?" I asked, "you see her much?"

"My mother?" His face changed to an expression of disgust—no, more like 'disappointment'—a sad flicker of his eyes gave it all away.

"They divorced?" I said.

"Yeah, when I was eight."

"Oh well, what's new? Most parents get divorced. Sticking together is pretty rare." I took a swig of Coke, hoping I didn't sound too cavalier. "What happened?"

He let out a deep sigh, "In a nutshell? She's an alcoholic. In all these years she's never cleaned up her act."

"Oh. Well, I can relate to that."

"Yeah, I suppose you can."

"I'm not talking about *myself*—I mean my mom."

"Your mum's a drinker?"

"*Was*. She died a long time ago. Well, actually, her drug of choice wasn't drink *exclusively*—she was more into pill popping."

He frowned. "I'm sorry you lost your mum—must have been tough."

"And yours? Where's she now?"

"In England. She lives in a small village in the

countryside. My dad still supports her—supports her habit, rather."

"But she managed to raise you, all the same?—get you to school, make your meals? You turned out okay. *Just*," I added jokily.

Jake snickered. "God, no. I was sent to boarding school—I was eight—they take boys as young as that in the UK. Tradition. Character building, you know? Then in the holidays—vacation time—I came to Los Angeles to be with my father and whoever happened to be his wife at the time. He went through a string of them."

"Nice." This felt good. Finally we were communicating, getting to know one another.

"Yup. Well, you know, I got my training to be a director that way. Plenty of drama all around, even off set. There was a ball-buster lawyer from Long Island who spoke through her nose, an Italian who had a Chihuahua she used to carry around in her handbag, a skinny Polish woman who used to pinch us when my dad wasn't looking, a gold digger from Iowa who wore false eyelashes that used to fall into her soup, and a Jamaican beauty queen called Rebecca. She—

Rebecca, I didn't forget in a hurry."

"Because she was beautiful?"

"Because I lost my virginity to her."

My Coca Cola went down the wrong way and I spluttered, "Your dad's *wife*? How old were you and how old was *she*?"

"I was fourteen. Guess she must have been a good ten years older."

"And you were okay with that? I mean, sneaking around behind your dad's back? I'm assuming he didn't *know* about it?"

"He was away on location for the best part of a year and was shagging someone else. Who was I to turn down beautiful Rebecca's advances?"

His story was amazingly "normal"—by Hollywood standards, anyway. I'd heard worse case-scenarios.

"This town is so screwed up," I murmured. "So then what happened? What became of Rebecca the beauty queen?"

"She must have gone back home. I remember lots of fighting and arguments. My dad isn't an easy man to live with."

"Powerful men can be difficult. Especially

when they're disobeyed."

"And megalomaniacs worse."

I locked my eyes with his. "And you? Has it rubbed off on you? Are *you* a 'megalomaniac'?"

He threaded his hand agitatedly through his hair. "I like to be in control."

"Don't we all."

"And that's why this is so hard for me, Star—because I'm losing it with you." He slipped his hand up along my thigh. Very slowly. My breath hitched at the suddenness of it all. I hadn't been expecting this. Just five minutes ago he didn't want anything to do with me.

"You see, I don't know how much longer I can hold out," he said in his cool English voice—so husky, so gravely—still with his hand on my leg. He leaned in closer, his messy hair flopping over his face.

I closed my eyes and couldn't help but let my senses go. His fingertips explored the soft flesh of my upper thigh and his thumb brushed past my panties, scraping the fabric of the cotton.

"You're wet, baby," he murmured.

"I'm not your baby." It came out as a growl,

but soon that growl turned into a purr—what he was doing felt sooo good, so sensual, I couldn't slap his hand away. I arched my back so I was closer to him. It was true; I was slippery wet. I felt two long fingers ease their way inside me and I moaned quietly. Then his thumb pressed onto my clit as he slid his fingers in and out. I heard a guttural groan coming deep from within him, reverberating in his strong chest where I laid my head. All he had on was his swim shorts—the towel having lost itself at some point—shot loose earlier by the strength of his rock-hard boner, which must have pinged it out of the way like a catapult.

We still hadn't kissed. Romance was obviously the last thing on his mind. He thought he had me—thought he had me all worked out. The One Sure Thing. Star Davis: the easy one who'd fuck any hot guy in the blink of an eye.

How wrong he was. And I couldn't wait to see his face when I told him.

And watch him sweat it out.

Just like all the others.

PRODUCTION
Shooting Star

DIRECTOR
Jake Wild

DATE
May

SCENE
What the fuck??

TAKE
10

CAMERA
Jake Wild

MY COCK WAS ON FIRE. Two weeks of pent up energy—I had a serious case of blue balls. And here was probably the sexiest, most beautiful woman I had ever known (and fuck, I'd known a lot) languidly inviting me to give it to her, right there, right then. Coming on to me for days, now. Tempting me by degrees. And I was burning. We both were. She was hotter than Hades, her long lean legs splayed beautifully across the couch, her tight wet pussy welcoming my fingers as I drove them in and out of her slowly, building her up to what I knew was going to be one long mind-blowing fuck and explosive climax.

I edged my way closer and with my other hand cupping her chin, I took in the vision of her beautiful face. There it was again; innocence mixed with a sort of wicked gleefulness. I moved my hand carefully up to the pearl of her ear, threading my fingers through her luscious, thick blond hair and took a fistful of it in my hand, bringing her face close to mine and resting my lips on hers. She let out a whimper and parted her mouth. I could smell her—all of her: strawberries, flowers, sex, her soft minty lips touching mine and, although I wanted to jump her immediately, there was something unexpectedly sensual about prolonging the kiss. She blinked at me—that guilelessness again—confounding me, confusing me—and sending shivers through my body—blood rushing to my groin. I was huge. I could feel her breath on my lips. I touched my tongue quietly with hers, just the tips as if we were teenagers—and a bolt of electricity shot straight to my rock-hard dick. Fuck! Now that I thought about it, she *was* still a teenager! *Jesus*! Still only nineteen. Practically jail bait. And however much she'd screwed around—

which I knew she had—I still needed to respect that. But I couldn't. I brushed my tongue along the seam of her full lips and flashes of fucking her on the sofa, on the floor, up against the wall, then in the shower, had me moaning into her mouth, my tongue tangling with hers, probing her, invading her.

She grabbed my hair as we breathed each other in. "You're beautiful, Jake," she said. My cock flexed at her sweet words and my hand slid down the base of her neck, across her slim shoulder, down to her pert breast. My fingers found her hard nipple, which I rolled between my thumb and forefinger, pulling at it hungrily. She groaned. She thrust her hips forward and I traced my fingers down her smooth taut stomach to her hot pussy. I plunged my fingers inside her slit and felt her liquid heat. My mouth latched onto her tit and I sucked greedily, then let go and flicked my tongue on her teat as she screamed out.

"Oh, God, Jake!"

"Fuck, you're sexy," I groaned, breathing in her sweet scent, nuzzling my head down, down, further down—licking as I went. I could smell her;

sweet and salty. I took out my fingers and pushed her legs wide apart, delving into her with my nose, letting my tongue circle her hard nub, round and around until she was crying out for me. I could tell she couldn't wait for my cock to split her open and fuck her good and hard.

My hands cupped her worked-out butt as I brought her close to me. Tantalizing her soaked center was turning me on like crazy. Alternating between fucking her with my tongue and flicking it on her clit, I lifted her hips to my face as she rocked her hips back and forth at me.

"This feels incredible, Jake. Oh God. You're amazing."

She'd fucked so many guys and I knew I was going to be just another notch on her bedpost. We were birds of a feather. But shit, I didn't care. Well, I did, but my dick didn't. He wanted to get off. Release himself into her tight little haven. He had a personality of his own. A brain of his own and all he was saying was, *Make her scream, make her come, then fuck her and make her come again.*

Star continued rocking her hips back and forth, fucking my mouth. I pressed my tongue flat against her clit as she slammed herself against me. "I'm gonna come," she whimpered.

Knowing I was giving her so much pleasure was making me harder than I think I'd ever been before. Huge, throbbing, thick and wide—in a few seconds I'd ram her full and fuck her till she detonated all over me. She was groaning now and started coming on my tongue, I could feel her contractions as she grabbed my head with her hands, thrashing about beneath me, screaming my name.

When she'd finished moaning and was easing into a blissful after-cum stupor, I edged my way onto the sofa, pinning her beneath me, my knees either side of her thighs.

"I'm going to really fuck you now, Star. Are you ready, baby?"

Her eyelids fluttered as if she was high on drugs—out of it—in her post-orgasmic rush. I slipped myself between her hot, sticky thighs and the huge crown of my cock throbbed at her entrance. I'd start slowly, I'd fuck her clit until she'd beg me to thrust all of myself into her. Hard. It felt so good as I slipped in a millimeter.

But suddenly she "awoke" with a start, her thighs clamping me with invincible strength like some super hero—Lara Croft—a cartoon character with inhuman powers. "Oh no you don't, Mr. Director." She levered me off her, her hands pushing hard at my shoulders.

Confusion danced in my sex-crazed brain. She wasn't fucking joking.

"What the hell's wrong, Star?"

"Party's over, Jake. I'm serious—this is as far as I go."

"What the fuck?" I said, and Dick screamed even louder at me, *Yeah, what the fuck, man*????

"I'm a virgin," Star whispered.

I laughed. "Yeah right. And pigs can fly!"

Star gave me another push. "I'm not kidding around. I'm a virgin, Jake!" Her eyes were moist and she looked terrified. Of me. Like I could rape her or something. A tear slid down her cheek. Was this for real? Or was she acting?

I shook my head. Of all the stories and rumors I'd heard about Star Davis, this was something I had not imagined in my wildest dreams. And when I say "Wildest" I'm aware of my play on words.

"But—"

She cut me off. "I'm not the person you hear about on the news, Jake Wild. Fooling around is one thing. But I don't actually *fuck*. Not you, not anybody. My chastity is precious. More precious than any movie negotiation, and certainly more precious than any short-lived relationship."

My face twisted into a contorted mess of bewilderment. "But—" I couldn't even finish my sentence. *What the hell is she playing at, going around being such a prick teaser?*

"*Why?*" I rasped, unable to process my thoughts. That was my only question: Why, why, *why*? What was in it for her to have a reputation for being so promiscuous?

"My mom gave me a really sound piece of advice. She said, 'Star, you can sell your talent but you must never sell either (a) your soul, or (b) your virginity because those two things are one-time offers. And you'd better make damn sure that the only person taking your soul is the Lord himself, and the only person taking your virginity is the man who'll love you unconditionally and eternally. No negotiation. Amen.' "

Jesus, she's some fucking religious nutter, born-again freak! I said nothing. Was this girl for *real*? I eyed her up lasciviously. Her skimpy, non-outfit riding up her thighs, her tussled mane of hair cascading over her shoulders, her pouting lips—all designed to conquer men. Her sex appeal was not just by accident. She worked on it, nurtured it.

She raised her brows haughtily. "You want me?" she challenged.

Yes, I fucking wanted her. Course I did. I was on fire. I'd sampled the goods and they were . . . delicious. I was hooked. Already obsessed. Knowing she was no longer "on offer" made her all the more tantalizing. The male mind—want what you can't have: a cliché, for sure. But fuck! I simply couldn't go there. A nineteen-year-old was bad enough, but a *virgin*? A virgin, prick-teasing control freak who was playing major head games with those around her. Star was now "hard to get" and like most spurned men snared in that category, I was caught in her Black Widow web. What a fool I was. My breath was short, my heart pounding like a lion cornering his kill but with a hunter at my side, after *me*. The hunter being Star herself. Diana.

Artemis. With a fucking bow and arrow at my throat. Moral blackmail, in a word.

"You want me?" she echoed, running her tongue along her soft lips—those beautiful red lips that I'd kissed only moments before. She eased her way up the sofa, still pushing me off her and she sat up. Double messages. So tantalizing. So luscious. But pure as the driven fucking snow. She flicked her head cockily, her blond mane tossed aside the way she was tossing *me* aside like used Kleenex. She'd had her fun. Satiated. Satisfied— her orgasm having ripped through her body like the seventh wave while I was still drooling for more like a dog hoping for a meager scrap.

But I couldn't let on that she had got to me. And I needed to overcome Dick's desire and walk away. *Now.* Before it was too late. I couldn't take on the responsibilities of a virgin. It would end in tears. I'd break her heart somewhere along the line and, yes, I was a commitment-phobe-sex-addict. A recipe for trouble with women who wanted "more." *And let's face it, all women want more.*

As I regarded her incredulously, still wondering if her "virgin" talk was a load of crap,

Star went on, "If you want me Jake—I mean *really* want me? You're going to have to work a *lot* harder and prove to me you're worthy, which I very much doubt you are, by the way."

"Worthy? Worthy enough for you?" I chuckled. Man, was she full of herself.

"Yes, that's right. My name *is* Star, after all. And I live up to my name."

I sat up. "Don't worry, babe. You can keep your precious virginity." I winked at her. "Keep it safe from me because I'm way too bad for you. My name *is* Wild. And I live up to *my* name." I said this, meaning it. But my cock—Dick Dastardly (or rather, Dick Bastardly), with his dumb, one-track "brain" of his own, had different ideas. He wanted Star. Badly. But I, Jake, had to be strong.

Because if I wasn't careful Star and I would end up playing a dangerous game of cat and mouse.

Brian was right: she and I had met our match.

And that match, I feared, was about to be struck and cause one hell of a fire . . .

To Be Continued . . .

Book 2, ***Falling Star***, out now

Thank you so much for choosing ***Shooting Star*** to be part of your library and I hope you enjoyed reading it as much as I enjoyed writing it. If you loved this book and have a minute please write a quick review. It helps authors so much. I am thrilled that you chose my book to be part of your busy life and hope to be re-invited to your bookshelf with my next release.

If you haven't read my other books I would love you to give them a try. The Pearl Series is a set of five, full-length erotic romance novels. I have also written a suspense novel, *Stolen Grace*.

The Pearl Trilogy
(all three books in one big volume)

Shades of Pearl
Shadows of Pearl
Shimmers of Pearl
Pearl
Belle Pearl

Join me on Facebook
(facebook.com/AuthorArianneRichmonde)

Join me on Twitter
(@A_Richmonde)

For more information about me, visit my website
(www.ariannerichmonde.com).

If you would like to email me:
ariannerichmonde@gmail.com

39401805R00073

Made in the USA
Middletown, DE
13 January 2017